The Evening News

Winner of

THE FLANNERY O'CONNOR AWARD

FOR SHORT FICTION

The Evening News

Stories by Tony Ardizzone

The University of Georgia Press
Athens and London

© 1986 by Tony Ardizzone
Published by the University of Georgia Press
Athens, Georgia 30602
All rights reserved

Set in Linotron 202 Times Roman
The paper in this book meets the guidelines for
permanence and durability of the Committee on
Production Guidelines for Book Longevity of the
Council on Library Resources

Printed in the United States of America

90 89 88 87 86   5 4 3 2 1

Library of Congress Cataloging in Publication Data

Ardizzone, Tony.
  The evening news.

    I. Title.
PS3551.R395E9   1986   813'.54   86-1403
ISBN 0-8203-0860-9 (alk. paper)

FOR DIANE KONDRAT

Acknowledgments

The author and the publisher gratefully acknowledge the magazines in which stories in this volume first appeared.

Beloit Fiction Journal: "The Eyes of Children"
Black Warrior Review: "My Mother's Stories" and "My Father's Laugh" (under the title "But You Can Call Me Thaddeus")
Carolina Quarterly: "Idling"
Epoch: "The Evening News" and "Nonna"
Memphis State Review: "World Without End"
The Minnesota Review: "The Intersection"
Quartet: "The Walk-On"
Seattle Review: "The Transplant"
The Texas Quarterly: "The Daughter and the Tradesman"

The author also wishes to thank the Old Dominion University Research Foundation for a summer fellowship that enabled him to complete work on this book.

Contents

My Mother's Stories   1

The Eyes of Children   14

The Evening News   25

My Father's Laugh   44

The Daughter and the Tradesman   70

Idling   83

The Transplant   92

The Intersection   106

World Without End   117

The Walk-On   128

Nonna   147

The Evening News

My Mother's Stories

They were going to throw her away when she was a baby. The doctors said she was too tiny, too frail, that she wouldn't live. They performed the baptism right there in the sink between their pots of boiling water and their rows of shining instruments, chose who would be her godparents, used water straight from the tap. Her father, however, wouldn't hear one word of it. He didn't listen to their *she'll only die anyway* and *please give her to us* and *maybe we can experiment*. No, the child's father stood silently in the corner of the room, the back of one hand wiping his mouth and thick mustache, his blue eyes fixed on the black mud which caked his pants and boots.

Nein, he said, finally. *Nein, die anyvay.*

With this, my mother smiles. She enjoys imitating the man's thick accent. She enjoys the sounds, the images, the memory. Her brown eyes look past me into the past. She draws a quick breath, then continues.

You can well imagine the rest. How the farmer took his wife and poor sickly child back to his farm. How the child was nursed, coddled, fed cow's milk, straight from the tops of the buckets—the rich, frothy cream. How the child lived. If she hadn't, I wouldn't be here now in the corner of this room, my eyes fixed on her, my mother and her stories. For now the sounds and pictures are *my* sounds and pictures. Her memory, my memory.

I stand here, remembering. The family moved. To Chicago, the city by the Great Lake, the city of jobs, money, opportunity. Away from northwestern Ohio's flat fields. The child grew. She is a young girl now, enrolled in school, Saint Teresa's, virgin. Chicago's Near North Side. The 1930s. And she is out walking with her girlfriend, a dark Sicilian. Spring, late afternoon. My mother wears a small pink bow in her brown hair.

Then from across the black pavement of the school playground comes a lilting stream of foreign sound, language melodic, of the kind sung solemnly at High Mass. The Sicilian girl turns quickly, smiling. The voice is her older brother's, and he too is smiling as he stands inside the playground fence. My mother turns but does not smile. She is modest. Has been properly, strictly raised. Is the last of seven children and, therefore, the object of many scolding eyes and tongues. Her name is Mary.

Perhaps our Mary, being young, is somewhat frightened. The boy behind the high fence is older than she, is in high school, is finely muscled, dark, deeply tanned. Around his neck hang golden things glistening on a thin chain. He wears a sleeveless shirt—his undershirt. Mary doesn't know whether to stay with her young friend or to continue walking. She stays, but she looks away from the boy's dark eyes and gazes instead at the worn belt around his thin waist.

That was my parents' first meeting. His name is Tony, as is mine. This is not a story she tells willingly, for she sees nothing special in it. All of the embellishments are mine. I've had to drag the story out of her, nag her from room to room. Ma? Ask your father, she tells me. I ask my father. He looks up from his newspaper, then starts to smile. He's in a playful mood. He laughs, then says: I met your mother in Heaven.

She, in the hallway, overhears. Bull, she says, looking again past me. He didn't even know I was alive. My father laughs behind his newspaper. I was Eva's friend, she says, and we were walking home from school—. I watch him, listening as he lowers the paper to look at her. She tells the story.

She knows how to tell a pretty good story, I think. She's a natural. She knows how to use her voice, when to pause, how to pace, what expressions to mask her face with. Her hand slices out the high fence. She's not in the same room with you when she really gets at it; her stories take her elsewhere, somewhere back. She's there again, back on a 1937 North Side sidestreet. My father and I are only witnesses.

Picture her, then. A young girl, frightened, though of course for no good reason—my father wouldn't have harmed her. I'll vouch for him. I'm his first son. But she didn't know that as the afternoon light turned low and golden from between distant buildings. Later she'd think him strange and rather arrogant, flexing his tanned muscles before her inside the fence, like a bull before a heifer. And for years (wasted ones, I think) she didn't give him a second thought, or so she claims—the years that she dated boys who were closer to her kind. These are her words.

Imagine those years, years of *ja Fräulein, ja, bitte, entschuldigen Sie,* years of pale Johnnys and freckled Fritzes and hairy Hermans, towheads all, who take pretty Mary dancing and roller-skating and sometimes downtown on the El to the movie theaters on State Street to see Clark Gable, and who buy popcorn and ice cream for her and, later, cups of coffee which she then drank with cream, and who hold her small hand and look up at the Chicago sky as they walk with her along the dark city streets to her father's flat on Fremont. Not *one* second thought? I cannot believe it. And whenever I interrupt to ask, she waves me away like I'm an insect flying between her eyes and what she really sees. I fold my arms, but I listen.

She was sweeping. This story always begins with that detail. With broom in hand. Nineteen years old and employed as a milliner and home one Saturday and she was sweeping. By now both her parents were old. Her mother had grown round, ripe like a fruit, like she would. Her father now fashioned wood. A mound of fluff and sawdust grows in the center of the room and she is humming, perhaps something from Glenn Miller, or she might have sung, as I've heard her do while ironing on the back porch, when from behind the locked back screen door there was suddenly a knock and it was my father, smiling.

She never tells the rest of the details. But this was the afternoon he proposed. Why he chose that afternoon, or even afternoon at all, are secrets not known to me. I ask her and she evades me. *Ask your father*. I ask him and he says he doesn't know. Then he looks at her and laughs, his eyes smiling, and I can see that he is making up some lie to tell me. I watch her. Because I loved her so much I couldn't wait until that night, he says. My mother laughs and shakes her head. No, he says, I'll tell you the truth this time. Now you really know he's lying. I was just walking down the street and the idea came to me. See, it was awful hot. His hand on his forehead, he pretends he had sunstroke. My mother laughs less.

There were problems. Another of her stories. They follow one after the next like cars out on the street—memories, there is just no stopping them. Their marriage would be mixed. Not in the religious sense—that would have been unthinkable— but in terms of language, origin, tradition. Like mixing your clubs with your hearts, mixing this girl from Liechtenstein with this boy from Sicily. Her family thought she was, perhaps, lowering herself. An Italian? Why not your kind? And his family, likewise, felt that he would be less than happy with a non-Sicilian girl. She's so skinny, they told him. *Misca!* Mary's skin and bones. When she has the first baby she'll bleed to death. And what will she feed you? Cabbages? *Marry your own kind.*

At their Mass someone failed to play "Ave Maria." Since that was the cue for my mother to stand and then to place a bouquet of flowers on Mary's side altar, she remained at the center altar, still kneeling, waiting patiently for the organist to begin. He was playing some other song, not "Ave Maria." The priest gestured to her. My mother shook her head. She was a beautiful bride, and she wore a velvet dress. You should see the wedding photograph that hangs in the hallway of their house in Chicago. Imagine a slender brown-haired bride in white velvet shaking her head at the priest who's just married her. No, the time is not yet for the young woman to stand, for her to kneel in prayer before the altar of the Virgin. This is her wedding day, remember. She is waiting for "Ave Maria."

She is waiting to this day, for the organist never did play the song, and the priest again motioned to her, then bent and whispered in her ear, and then, indignant, crushed, the young bride finally stood and angrily, solemnly, sadly waited for her maid of honor to gather the long train of her flowing velvet dress, and together the two marched to the Virgin's side altar.

She tells this story frequently, whenever there is a wedding. I think that each time she begins the story she is tempted to change the outcome, to make the stupid organist suddenly stop and slap his head. To make the organist begin the chords of "Ave Maria." That kind of power isn't possible in life. The organist didn't stop or slap his head.

I wonder if the best man tipped him. If my father was angry enough to complain. If the muscles in his jaws tightened, if his hands turned to fists, if anyone waited for the organist out in the parking lot. I am carried away.

Details *are* significant. Literally they can be matters of life and death. An organist makes an innocent mistake in 1946 and for the rest of her life a woman is compelled to repeat a story, as if for her the moment has not yet been fixed, as if by remembering and then speaking she could still influence the pattern of events since passed.

Life and death—
I was hoping the counterpart wouldn't be able to work its

way into this story. But it's difficult to keep death out. The final detail. Always coming along unexpectedly, the uninvited guest at the banquet, acting like you were supposed to have known all along that he'd get there, expecting to be seated and for you to offer him a drink.

My father called yesterday. He said he was just leaving work to take my mother again to the hospital. Tests. I shouldn't call her yet. No need to alarm her, my father said. Just tests. We'll keep you posted. My mother is in the hospital. I am not Meursault.

I must describe the counterpart, return, begin again. With 1947, with my mother, delirious, in labor. Brought to the hospital by my father early on a Saturday, and on Monday laboring still. The doctors didn't believe in using drugs. She lay three days, terrified, sweating. On Monday morning they brought my father into the room, clad in an antiseptic gown, his face covered by a mask. She mistook him for one of the doctors. When he bent to kiss her cheek she grabbed his arm and begged him. Doctor, doctor, can you give me something for the pain?

That Monday was Labor Day. Ironies exist. Each September now, on my older sister Diana's birthday, my mother smiles and tells that story.

Each of us was a difficult birth. Did my father's family know something after all? The fourth, my brother Bob, nearly killed her. He was big, over ten pounds. The doctors boasted, proudly, that Bob set their personal record. The fifth child, Jim, weighed almost ten-and-a-half pounds, and after Jim the doctors fixed my mother so that there wouldn't be a sixth child. I dislike the word *fixed,* but it's an appropriate word, I think.

When I was a child my mother once took Diana and me shopping, to one of those mom-and-pop stores in the middle of the block. I remember a blind man who always sat on a wooden milk crate outside the store with his large dog. I was afraid of the dog. Inside the store we shopped, and my mother told us stories, and the three of us were laughing. She lifted a carton of soda as she spoke. Then the rotted cardboard bottom of the carton gave way and the soda bottles fell. The bottles burst. The sharp glass bounced. She shouted and we screamed, and as she tells this story she makes a point of remembering how worried she was that the glass had reached our eyes. But then some woman in the store told her she was bleeding. My mother looked down. Her foot was cut so badly that blood gushed from her shoe. I remember the picture, but then the face of the blind man's dog covers up the image and I see the wooden milk crate, the scratched white cane.

The middle child, Linda, is the special one. It was on a Christmas morning when they first feared she was deaf. Either Diana or I knocked over a pile of toy pans and dishes—a pretend kitchen—directly behind the one-year-old child playing on the floor, and Linda, bright and beautiful, did not move. She played innocently, unaffected, removed from the sound that had come to life behind her. Frantic, my mother then banged two of the metal dinner plates behind Linda's head. Linda continued playing, in a world by herself, softly cooing.

What I can imagine now from my mother's stories is a long procession of doctors, specialists, long trips on the bus. Snow-covered streets. Waiting in sterile waiting rooms. Questions. Answers. More questions. Tests. Hope. Then, no hope. Then guilt came. Tony and Mary blamed themselves.

Forgive the generalities. She is a friendly woman; she likes to make others laugh. Big-hearted, perhaps to a fault, my mother has a compulsion to please. I suspect she learned that trait as a child, being the youngest of so many children. Her parents were quite old, and as I piece her life together I imagine them strict, resolute, humorless. My mother would disagree were she to hear me. But I suspect that she's been bullied and made to feel inferior, by whom or what I don't exactly know, and, to compensate, she works very hard at pleasing.

She tells a story about how she would wash and wax her oldest brother's car and how he'd pay her one penny. How each day, regardless of the weather, she'd walk to a distant newsstand and buy for her father the *Abendpost*. How she'd be sent on especially scorching summer days by another of her brothers for an ice cream cone, and how as she would gingerly carry it home she'd take not one lick. How could she resist? In my mother's stories she's always the one who's pleasing.

Her brown eyes light up, and like a young girl she laughs. She says she used to cheat sometimes and take a lick. Then, if her brother complained, she'd claim the ice cream had been melted by the sun. Delighted with herself, she smiles. Her eyes again twinkle with light.

I am carried away again. If it were me in that story I'd throw the cone to the ground and tell my brother to get his own damn ice cream.

You've seen her. You're familiar with the kind of house she lives in, the red brick two-flat. You've walked the tree-lined city street. She hangs the family's wash up in the small backyard, the next clothespin in her mouth. She picks up the squashed paper cups and the mustard-stained foot-long hot dog wrappers out in the front that the kids from the public school leave behind as they walk back from the Tastee-Freeze on the corner. During the winter she sweeps the snow. Wearing a discarded pair of my father's earmuffs. During the fall she sweeps leaves. She gets angry when the kids cut through the backyard, leaving the chain-link gates open, for the dog barks then and the barking bothers her. The dog, a female schnauzer mutt, is called Alfie. No ferocious beast—the plastic BEWARE OF DOG signs on the gates have the harsher bite. My mother doesn't like it when the kids leave the alley gate open. She talks to both her neighbors across both her fences. Wearing one of Bob's old sweaters, green and torn at one elbow, she bends to pick up a fallen autumn twig. She stretches to hang

the wash up—the rows of whites, then the coloreds. She lets
Alfie out and checks the alley gate.

Summer visit. Over a mug of morning coffee I sit in the
kitchen reading the *Sun-Times*. Alfie in the backyard barks and
barks. My mother goes outside to quiet her. I turn the page,
reading of rape or robbery, something distant. Then I hear the
dog growl, then again bark. I go outside.

My mother is returning to the house, her face red, angry.
Son of a B, she says. I just caught some punk standing outside
the alley gate teasing Alfie. She points. He was daring her to
jump at him, and the damn kid was holding one of the garbage
can lids over his head, just waiting to hit her. My mother dem-
onstrates with her hands.

I run to the alley, ready to fight, to defend. But there is no
one in the alley.

My mother stands there on the narrow strip of sidewalk, her
hands now at her sides. She looks tired. Behind her in the yard
is an old table covered with potted plants. Coleus, philodendron, wandering Jew. One of the planters, a statue of the
Sacred Heart of Jesus. Another, Mary with her white ceramic
hands folded in prayer. Mother's Day presents of years ago.
Standing in the bright morning sun.

And when I came out, my mother continues, the punk just
looked at me, real snotty-like, like he was *daring* me, and then
he said come on and hit me, lady, you just come right on and
hit me. I'll show you, lady, come on. And then he used the *F*
word. She shakes her head and looks at me.

Later, inside, as she irons one of my father's shirts, she tells
me another story. It happened last week, at night. The ten
o'clock news was on. Time to walk Alfie. She'd been feeling
lousy all day so Jim took the dog out front instead.

So he was standing out there waiting for Alfie to finish up
her business when all of a sudden he hears this engine and he
looks up, and you know what it was, Tony? Can you guess, of
all things? It was this car, this *car*, driving right down along

the sidewalk with its lights out. Jim said he dove straight for the curb, pulling poor Alfie in the middle of number two right with him. And when they went past him they swore at him and threw an empty beer can at him. She laughs and looks at me, then stops ironing and sips her coffee. Her laughter is from fear. Well, you should have heard your little brother when he came back in. Boy was he steaming! They could have killed him they were driving so fast. The cops caught the kids up at Tastee-Freeze corner. We saw the squad car lights from the front windows. It was a good thing Jim took the dog out that night instead of me. She sprinkles the shirt with water from a Pepsi bottle. Can you picture your old mother diving then for the curb?

She makes a tugging gesture with her hands. Pulling the leash. Saving herself and Alfie. Again she laughs. She tells the story again when Jim comes home.

At first the doctors thought she had disseminated lupus erythematosus. Lupus means wolf. It is primarily a disease of the skin. As lupus advances, the victim's face becomes ulcerated by what are called butterfly eruptions. The face comes to resemble a wolf's. Disseminated lupus attacks the joints as well as the internal organs. There isn't a known cure.

And at first they made her hang. My mother. They made her buy a sling into which she placed her head, five times each day. Pulling her head from the other side was a heavy water bag. My father put the equipment up on the door of my bedroom. For years when I went to sleep I stared at that water bag. She had to hang for two-and-a-half hours each day. Those were the years that she read every book she could get her hands on.

And those were the years that she received the weekly shots, the cortisone, the steroids, that made her puff up, made her put on the weight the doctors are now telling her to get rid of.

Then one of the doctors died, and then she had to find new

doctors, and then again she had to undergo their battery of tests. These new doctors told her that she probably didn't have lupus, that instead they thought she had severe rheumatoid arthritis, that the ten years of traction and corticosteroids had been a mistake. They gave her a drugstore full of pills then. They told her to lose weight, to exercise each night. A small blackboard hangs over the kitchen sink. The markings put there each day appear to be Chinese. Long lines for these pills, dots for those, the letter *A* for yet another. A squiggly line for something else. The new doctors taught her the system. When you take over thirty pills a day you can't rely on memory.

My father called again. He said there was nothing new. Mary is in the hospital again, and she's been joking that she's somewhat of a celebrity. So many doctors come in each day to see her. Interns. Residents. They hold conferences around her bed. They smile and read her chart. They question her. They thump her abdomen. They move her joints. They point. One intern asked her when she had her last menstrual cycle. My mother looked at the young man, then at the other doctors around her bed, then smiled and said twenty-some years ago but I couldn't for the life of me tell you which month. The intern's face quickly reddened. My mother's hysterectomy is written there in plain view on her chart.

They ask her questions and she recites her history like a litany.

Were the Ohio doctors right? Were they prophets? *Please give her to us. Maybe we can experiment.*

My father and I walk along the street. We've just eaten, then gone to Osco for the evening paper—an excuse, really, just to take a walk. And he is next to me suddenly bringing up the subject of my mother's health, just as suddenly as the wind from the lake shakes the thin branches of the trees. The moment is serious, I realize. My father is not a man given to unnecessary talk.

I don't know what I'd do without her, he says. I say nothing, for I can think of nothing to say. We've been together for over thirty years, he says. He pauses. For nearly thirty-four years. Thirty-four years this October. And, you know, you wouldn't think it, but I love her so much more now. He hesitates, and I look at him. He shakes his head and smiles. You know what I mean? he says. I say yes and we walk for a while in silence, and I think of what it must be like to live with someone for thirty-four years, but I cannot imagine it, and then I hear my father begin to talk about that afternoon's ball game—he describes at length and in comic detail a misjudged fly ball lost in apathy or ineptitude or simply in the sun—and for the rest of our walk home we discuss what's right and wrong with our favorite baseball team, our thorn-in-the-side Chicago Cubs.

I stand here, not used to speaking about things that are so close to me. I am used to veiling things in my stories, to making things wear masks, to telling my stories through masks. But my mother tells her stories openly, as she has done so all of her life—since she lived on her father's farm in Ohio, as she walked along the crowded 1930 Chicago streets, to my father overseas in her letters, to the five of us children, as we sat on her lap, as we played in the next room while she tended to our supper in the kitchen. She tells them to everyone, to anyone who will listen. She taught Linda to read her lips.

I learn now to read her lips.

And I imagine one last story.

Diana and I are children. Our mother is still young. Diana and I are outside on the sidewalk playing and it's summer. And we are young and full of play and happy, and we see a dog, and it comes toward us on the street. My sister takes my hand. She senses something, I think. The dog weaves from side to side. It's sick, I think. Some kind of lather is on its mouth. The dog growls. I feel Diana's hand shake.

Now we are inside the house, safe, telling our mother. Linda, Bob, and Jim are there. We are all the same age, all children. Our mother looks outside, then walks to the telephone. She returns to the front windows. We try to look out the windows too, but she pushes the five of us away.

No, she says. I don't want any of you to see this.

We watch her watching. Then we hear the siren of a police car. We watch our mother make the sign of the Cross. Then we hear a shot. Another. I look at my sisters and brothers. They are crying. Worried, frightened, I begin to cry too.

Did it come near you? our mother asks us. Did it touch you? Any of you? Linda reads her lips. She means the funny dog. Or does she mean the speeding automobile with its lights off? The Ohio doctors? The boy behind the alley gate? The shards of broken glass? The wolf surrounded by butterflies? The ten-and-a-half-pound baby?

Diana, the oldest, speaks for us. She says that it did not.

Our mother smiles. She sits with us. Then our father is with us. Bob cracks a smile, and everybody laughs. Alfie gives a bark. The seven of us sit closely on the sofa. Safe.

That actually happened, but not exactly in the way that I described it. I've heard my mother tell that story from time to time, at times when she's most uneasy, but she has never said what it was that she saw from the front windows. A good storyteller, she leaves what she has all too clearly seen to our imaginations.

I stand in the corner of this room, thinking of her lying now in the hospital.

I pray none of us looks at that animal's face.

The Eyes of Children

The two seventh-grade girls came running to the playground, their pink cheeks streaked with tears, the pleated skirts of their navy-blue uniforms snapping in the wind. It was a windy Friday. Some of the children looked at the sky to see if it would rain. They gathered in loose bunches by the gate near Sister Immaculata, the sixth-grade teacher, her skirts swirling like a child's pennant caught in a stiff breeze. The black folds of her habit whipped away behind her, flapping toward the gate and the alleyway, now shifting as the wind shifted, as she turned to face the wind. Dry leaves and scraps of paper whirled in circles on the ground beneath the basketball hoops. Dust stung the children's eyes. Not even Patrick Riley, the tallest eighth-grader and captain of the basketball team, risked trying a shot against the wind. He sat on the parish basketball against the fence, flanked by his teammates who chewed their fingernails or stood, hands in pockets, turning into the wind like Sister Immaculata.

Gino Martini, a dark seventh-grader, knew he would have tried a shot. He stood near the players, fighting a yawn, his skinny arms folded across his chest. If he had the ball, he'd put it up. The ball would fall cleanly through the chain net, and everyone would cheer him. A yellowed sheet of newspaper rose suddenly in the air and slammed into the playground fence, spreading flat against the weave of chain link. Gino was sleepy from serving the week's 6:45 morning Masses. He stared at a light-haired girl whose name he didn't know, watching how the wind pressed her skirt back against her legs. The blonde girl was pretty and stood all by herself, but Gino was shy and she was an eighth-grader. The only seventh-grade boys the eighth-grade girls talked to were the guys on the school team. Gino had wanted to be on the team, but his father insisted he work after school, to learn responsibility, the value of a dollar. His mother insisted he serve God by being an altar boy. He had to obey. But no one knew him. The pretty girl didn't look at him, and Mrs. Bagnola and Sister Bernadette walked past her toward Sister Immaculata, and Mrs. Bagnola looked at her wristwatch and shook her head. The wind blew. Traffic rushed by in the street. Someday, Gino thought, I'll be part of something wonderful someday. Then everyone heard the cries of the two girls who ran inside the fence bordering the playground, and the girls grabbed the arms of their teachers, and the children crowded around them, pushed by the wind.

"The church!" shouted Donna Pietro, sobbing against Bernadette's chest.

"He was there," Maureen Ostrowski screamed, "he was there, in the church!" Her hands squeezed Mrs. Bagnola's arm.

"There now," Bernadette said. She stroked Donna's dark hair. "Take deep breaths. You've frightened yourselves."

"We—" Donna cried. "We didn't do anything, Sister!"

"All of a sudden he was just there!" Maureen said. "And he was bleeding!"

"Who?" Mrs. Bagnola said. Her hands grasped Maureen's shoulders and shook them until the girl's eyes steadied.

"Start from the beginning," Sister Immaculata said.

Donna gulped a breath, then stared at the sky. "Maureen forgot her scarf, Sister, so after lunch we went to church."

"During choir practice, Sister," Maureen said. "This morning."

"Maureen left her scarf up in the loft during choir practice."

"It was my mother's—" Maureen stomped her foot. "And she didn't know I borrowed it." She began to cry.

"So you two went to the choir loft—" prodded Mrs. Bagnola.

"We should send someone to the rectory," Immaculata said.

"Not yet," Bernadette said. She looked at Mrs. Bagnola, then at the two girls. "You went up to the loft?"

"We didn't do anything, Sister!" Donna said. "Then all of a sudden he was there." She spread her arms and bent at the waist. "At the top of the loft by the stairs, just looking at us!" Donna again began to cry.

"Who?" Bernadette said.

"We thought he was Mr. Lindsey," Maureen said in a low voice. She wiped her tears with her fingertips. Mr. Lindsey was the parish choirmaster. "But he didn't say anything when we said hello—"

"We said, 'Good afternoon, Mr. Lindsey.' We only whispered."

"—and then he turned, and his face was horrible and bleeding." Maureen's lips quivered. She looked out at the street. "And he wouldn't move or anything. He just stood there, blood dripping from his face. We couldn't run because he was by the stairs. Donna screamed—"

"We both screamed, Sister."

"—and then he wasn't there anymore, and then we heard someone making noise downstairs in the church."

"Send a boy to the rectory," Bernadette told Mrs. Bagnola.

Gino waved his hand and bounced on his toes. Since he served so many Masses, it was only fair. But Mrs. Bagnola's eyes looked beyond him over the crush of children. She motioned to Patrick Riley.

"—down the steps," Maureen was saying. She held out her hand like she was grasping a railing. "And there were drops of blood on the marble—"

"Tiny drops of blood," Donna said. She shook herself. "—didn't step in them, Sister, because we were afraid! He was horrible, standing there by the stairs holding the door open like he wanted us to come to him. And behind him was the stained-glass window." Maureen made the sign of the Cross. Around Gino some of the children crossed themselves too.

"I didn't want to get any of the blood on my shoes," Donna said. "These are my only pair of good shoes!"

"It's all right, Donna," Sister Bernadette said. "Your shoes are fine."

"And in the window Jesus was looking down on us, pointing to His Sacred Heart. And all we could see then was that big window. All the colors. The bright light." Maureen looked into the distance.

"I'll throw them away," Donna said, lifting her feet. "Even if the blood just got on the bottom! I'll throw them in a furnace! They'll burn, won't they, Sister?"

"We'll clean your shoes in Mother Superior's office," Bernadette said.

Mrs. Bagnola stepped forward. "This man, he didn't say anything to you or do anything, did he?"

The girls didn't move, then stared at each other and shook their heads.

"Thank God," said Sister Immaculata.

Her words rippled through the children. Some girls nodded and grabbed one another's hands. Donna ground the bottoms of her shoes on the asphalt. Maureen held one arm at her side, her finger pointing to her heart. Then Mrs. Bagnola checked her watch and nodded to Immaculata and Bernadette, and Bernadette blew her whistle, and the children assembled in three lines that buzzed with talk. Sister Bernadette left the playground first, walking between Maureen and Donna, shrinking as she moved up the alley that led to the school. Already the little children were marching toward school from their smaller playground across the street. They sang a merry song as they marched. Gino watched everything, standing silently in line, thinking maybe there'd been a terrible car crash and the man had smashed his face against the windshield, then run to the church looking for a priest who'd give him the Last Rites. Gino wished Mrs. Bagnola had chosen him to go to the rectory. He wanted to see the drops of blood, and if they made a trail. If the priests followed the trail they'd find the man and could hear his confession. A girl in the front of Gino's line began to cry. Maybe she got a cinder in her eye, Gino thought. Sister Immaculata's group walked from the playground. The wind was blowing up lots of dust. The man was most likely waiting inside one of the confessionals, and right now Father Manning was probably forgiving all his sins. The girl wept, circled by other girls. It wasn't a big deal. Just a man and some blood. A stray mutt ran past the children nearest the fence. Mrs. Bagnola shooed the dog away, and the wind blew and bent the heads of the children, and Gino's line began the march up the alley to the school.

That afternoon passed slowly. All the seventh-graders stared at the fifth row, at the pair of empty desks. Mother Superior explained that Donna and Maureen had been given the afternoon off. Hands rose in the air. Mother Superior said there would be no discussion, and when she knelt next to the wooden platform beneath Sister Bernadette's desk and took out her rosary Gino realized they'd spend the afternoon praying. The children knelt, as noisily as falling blocks, on the wooden floor. When Sister Bernadette returned to her classroom Gino tried to read her face, but the woman was as somber and unreadable as Latin. Gino's class prayed three rosaries: one for Maureen, one for Donna, the third for the bleeding man.

"It's an unfortunate incident," Bernadette told the class. She stared at the clock on the wall. There were a few minutes before the bell.

"The church is a refuge for the sick and needy," Sister continued. "The doors of the parish are always open. The priests receive calls at all hours of the day and night. Once, at midnight, a poor woman knocked on the rectory door because she had no food to feed her hungry children and she was tempted to go out and steal, and the priests gave her food. Another time a very rich man was driving around in his limousine thinking of committing the unforgivable sin of suicide, because you know wealth does not bring a person peace or true happiness, and the priests listened to him and gave him their blessing, and the man renounced all his earthly belongings and went on to live a life dedicated to Christ." She smiled. "So you see, children, sometimes the church does have unhappy visitors, but God greets them all with forgiveness and love." Then the final bell sounded.

The sky looked like it would rain. Gino thought about Sister's words as he hurried home. Maybe, he thought, there wasn't a car accident. Maybe the man was just an unhappy visitor. But then why was he bleeding? Gino hoped it wouldn't rain until after he finished his paper route. Why was he bleeding? He heard a bouncing basketball and saw Patrick Riley and his friends standing inside the playground. The boys were talking loudly. They didn't answer Gino's shy hello. He walked slowly so he could hear what they said.

"—all over the Saint Joseph's side aisle," Patrick said. "Man alive, I couldn't believe it."

"Those girls were awful lucky," one boy said.

"Lucky?" another said. "Lucky ain't the word."

"Nobody knows what he would of done if he'd of caught them."

"He probably had a knife. Or a razor. Maybe a switchblade. He could of slit their throats."

"Nah."

"Sure. A strange guy bleeding all over the church? Whatdya think?"

"He sure wasn't there to make no Stations of the Cross."
The boys laughed.

Patrick bounced the ball. "Father Pinky said he was some
kind of lunatic. You know, out of his mind, not knowing what
he was doing."

"Rita Binetti and her friends were talking about him maybe
being a saint or something like that."

"I heard them. Felice Hernandez said maybe it was a vision. You know, like Our Lady of Guadalupe, or Lourdes."

"Then how could he leave behind all that blood?"

"Visions can bleed."

"No."

"Yeah."

"Yeah, maybe the blood can cure you if you touch it."

"Nah," Patrick said. "He was a lunatic."

"He could of been a miracle, you know. He didn't hurt
them. He had them trapped up in the choir loft. All they got
was a little scared."

"Rita said maybe he was Jesus."

"What's she know? Her brother is so stupid he flunked second grade."

Gino crossed the street, thinking of the two girls. Donna
scraping her shoes on the ground. Maureen holding her hand
to her chest, like the window of the Sacred Heart. Maureen
said she remembered the window because of the bright light.
But it was a cloudy day. Gino looked at the sky. Maybe he *was*
Jesus, Gino thought. And Jesus knew in His infinite wisdom
that Maureen would forget her mother's scarf, and the girls
would search the loft for it, and then He'd appear to them,
right beneath the stained-glass window so they'd know, and
He'd leave behind the trail of His Most Sacred Blood, and the
trail would lead. . . . Gino stared at the sidewalk. The trail
would lead to God the Father, of course. The boy walked
quickly now, excited by his thoughts. Maureen and Donna
were awful lucky to have been chosen, but like in all the other

visitation stories at first the people wouldn't believe them, and the priests and Church authorities would have to try to shake their faith. But in the end, after many miracles, everyone would believe them and the girls would be very holy, and after they died they'd be saints. Yes. Gino ran home now. He no longer cared if it rained. He wanted to hurry to the newspaper office to see if the news was on the front page. He'd believe in the miracle from the start. Yes, he would believe. No doubt. Already he believed.

His alarm clock woke him early the next morning. The sky behind his bedroom shade was dark. All the others were still sleeping, so Gino was quiet as he slipped his clothes off their hangers and then tiptoed to the bathroom to wash. He had time, he thought. He didn't need to rush. Usually the alarm would shriek for a full minute before he'd wake, but this morning he sat up in bed, aware, with the first ring. He was careful not to swallow any toothpaste as he brushed his teeth. He didn't want to break his Communion fast. Especially today, the first day after the miracle. In the kitchen he glanced at the clock, always set ten minutes fast so everyone would be on time. He left a note next to the bread on the table. I WENT TO SERVE. Slapping his pants pocket to make sure he had his house key, he grabbed his jacket. The front door lock clicked softly behind him.

Only a white milk truck moved down the street. Gino walked along the sidewalk darkened by the evening's rain. The night had seen a real storm. He stepped over flattened leaves, twigs, branches thick as his arm. There'd been plenty of lightning and low, rolling thunder, the kind that lasted many seconds and rattled the windowpanes and terrified Gino's younger brothers and sisters, but he hadn't been afraid. The storm was right, wonderful. Gino knew it stormed because the girls had seen Jesus in the church.

The miracle hadn't been in the newspaper. Gino had won-

dered why, then concluded that the people who printed the
newspaper weren't Catholics. At supper when he told his parents they'd misunderstood. No, he argued. No. You have to
believe! "Eat," his father had told him.

They'd see, Gino thought. And he would be special because
he knew and believed from the beginning. He walked past the
school, breathing the cool air that tasted wet and fresh from the
night's storm, then cut through the empty parish courtyard and
entered through the side doorway of the church.

The dark hallway leading to the altar boys' room stretched
ahead of him. He dipped his fingers into the holy water fount
and made the sign of the Cross. On the wooden floor by the
fount were pages torn from a parish hymnbook. Gino picked
them up, then saw the edge of another torn page crushed beneath the inner side door. What? He opened the inner door of
the church.

His breath tripped in his throat. Covering the marble floor
were scores of shattered vigil lights. They looked like they'd
been thrown there. The wrought-iron stand that had held them
lay on its side. More hymnals had been flung to the floor. Gino
looked at Mary's side altar. The blue embroidered cloth hanging over it had been slashed. The gold candlesticks were
knocked down, and each candle was broken. Flowers and
more vigil lights lay smashed on the altar's steps. The heavy
tabernacle beneath the statue of the Virgin had been tipped
from its base, as if shoved by a giant, and rested at a dizzy
angle. Glass crunched beneath his feet as he stepped forward.
He turned and ran.

Gino ran up the dark hallway to the altar boys' room. Pitch
black. His fingers found the light switch. Nothing there had
been damaged. No one else was there. He hurried down half
the length of the dark passageway that ran behind the center
altar and led to the sacristy and rectory, calling out, "Father!
Father!" But when he heard no response he stopped in the
darkness. He listened to his pounding heart. There was noth-

ing to do but return to the servers' room and dress for Mass.
Numbly, he took his black cassock from the closet. He threw
on his surplice. Then he buttoned the top button of his white
shirt. His fingers were shaking. Gino looked at his hands, then
genuflected and held them for a moment to his face.

Then he took a long breath and walked again down the passageway, hearing the echo of his footsteps. Someone was
there now—a priest, smoke curling from a cigarette.

"Father!" Gino cried. "Father, the church!"

"I know," Father Manning said, cinching the cord around
his alb.

"But, Father—"

The priest walked toward him and put his hand on his shoulder. "You'll forgive me. I don't usually smoke here. I don't
want to give you a bad example. You don't smoke, do you,
Gino?"

"No, Father." The hand still held his shoulder.

"Good. I wish I shared your self-control." The priest withdrew his arm.

"But the church—" Gino began.

"We'll clean up the mess before too many people see it.
Don't be upset."

"But I thought it was a miracle, Father."

"What?" Father Manning said.

Gino looked away, then at the priest's face. "I thought that
Maureen and Donna—"

Father Manning took a deep drag off his cigarette. "There
was nothing miraculous about what happened here." Smoke
streamed from his mouth. The priest turned to finish dressing.

Gino nodded, confused, events still piecing themselves together. He went to the wine closet for the cruets. Father Manning called out, "Full." So Gino filled one of the cruets with
wine, the other with cold water. The water splashed in the
sink. He set them next to the dish and cloth and patens that
rested on the table next to the altar, and then returned to the

sacristy for the long pole used to light the candles, and he lit the center pair, and tears welled in his eyes.

No miracle. A flush as burning as the flame washed over him. Fool. To try to be special. To believe. For a moment he stood quietly at the altar, holding the flame to the tall candle, feeling the tears drip from his cheeks to the altar cloth. Then a sudden sorrow fell over him. All at once the world seemed very dark and very big.

The Evening News

Their fears appear nightly, as routinely as the newscaster's face. Framed by the plastic black rectangle of the portable color television set Maria's parents had given them, the newscaster's head and shoulders normally fill two-thirds of the screen, and the man's face is always calm, pale salmon. Behind him is a soothing gray-blue backdrop. The other third of the picture is left to maps of Poland, El Salvador, the Falkland Islands. Paul wonders who chooses the colors for the maps. El Salvador is usually brown; Poland, nearly always red. Argentina is green and jagged. Paul likes to tinker with the knob labeled TONE to make the countries any color he wants them to be. Sometimes when Maria isn't in the room he turns down the BRIGHT knob and makes everything turn black. Paul's parents didn't have a color television when he was growing up. Whenever he watches baseball he likes the colors to be true, but not so gaudy that he is distracted by them. The grass in the infield has to be lime green, the dirt around home plate barely orange. Paul has been to Atlanta. The earth is barely orange in Atlanta. Atlanta is nearly five hundred miles away, but cable picks up all the televised games. The Braves now call themselves America's Team. During the first week they had the set Paul waited patiently for a shot of the American flag flying out in center field; then he quickly locked in the flag's red stripes, its square field of blue, its crisp wrinkled lines of white, then marked each knob with a Flair pen so he could always return the colors to where they were supposed to be, clearly there on the screen, bright and true, but not so loud as to be distracted by them.

Maria doesn't care about the color. When she turns on the TV set, any colors are all right with her, even black and white. Maria is seven months pregnant. The color set was a pregnancy gift. Each day when she comes home from the university library where she works she watches "General Hospital," her favorite soap opera, usually in black and white. She calls the soaps "the dopes." She hasn't smoked any marijuana since she learned she was pregnant. Though the baby wasn't planned, Maria takes all the right vitamins and eats enough protein and vegetables to make herself sometimes so sick of doing things right that she wants to roll a fat joint and get high, but she doesn't have any grass in the house and she knows that drugs are probably bad for the baby. She drinks red wine instead. Seldom more than seven glasses a week. Paul drinks a lot of wine, mostly imported, now that they can afford it. He grew up drinking inexpensive homemade wine. None of the expensive imported wine is as good as what he remembers drinking. He thinks of himself as ethnic. At a Sociology Department party he joked that America was a Wonder Bread culture, soft and white, slickly packaged with pictures of colorful balloons. You think you're holding something of integrity and substance, but when you squeeze it you have mostly preservatives and air. Maria doesn't know what to think of herself. Her Spanish isn't fluent, and she has never been to Mexico, where her grandparents were born. She always feels peculiar checking the box next to HISPANIC on the equal opportunity forms. Paul is much less American than she, and he has no box to check. Today he comes home unexpectedly early from his teaching job at the university and sees Luke Spencer's worried face on the screen in black and white, and he adjusts the knobs, making darker marks with his Flair pen. "Why don't you set this thing right?" he asks Maria. "Why do we have color if you don't use it?" "You're blocking the picture," Maria says. She tries to stare past him. "You make a better door than a window." Paul asks Maria if he can get her anything, if she felt O.K. at work, if she wants her feet or back rubbed. Maria waits until a commercial to tell him no, yes, no. He checks the morning newspaper to see if the Braves have an afternoon game. Today is an off-day. In the kitchen he pours a glass of apple juice. At the sink he rinses the evening's vegetables, then chops them at the table in the dining room. He sneaks behind Maria and kisses her on the cheek. He makes the salad and adds the imported black olives she hadn't seen him slip into the grocery cart. Paul likes doing things for Maria. He loves her, more than he knows, especially now that she is going to have a baby. This is a special, if tense, time in their lives—this spring, a year after the baseball strike, the year Paul is going up for tenure, the year Maria received a higher classification and a 5.2 percent raise at the library, the year they are learning Lamaze. Their afternoons together are cool and peaceful, and Luke Spencer is searching for his missing Laura, and the Braves are hot, on a winning streak. Yesterday the chairman of the department told Paul he needn't worry. Earlier in the week the obstetrician told Maria she was coming along just fine. The evening news won't be on for a few more hours. Paul readjusts the color of Luke's curly mop of hair as Maria chews a slice of celery and then closes her eyes and naps on the sofa facing the portable television.

Earlier that year they had a dog. Her name was Bingo, and she was a dumb mistake. An impulsive decision made in a shopping mall the day before Christmas Eve two years ago. Paul and Maria paused before a pet store window and predictably Paul said, "Look at the cute puppies." He had never had a dog. He hadn't bought Maria's present yet. A toddler in a harness and leash pulled his mother toward the window, pointing with a wet finger he'd just taken from his mouth. Beneath the vague noise of footsteps and muffled conversations a Christmas carol was playing. From the doorway of the store a salesman in a doctor's white lab coat smiled at Maria, then caught Paul's eye and winked.

Maria and Paul sat inside a paneled cubicle, and the man in the white doctor's coat brought them the smallest of the puppies swaddled in a clean white towel. The puppy trembled, then licked Maria's fingers. "He's so frightened," she said.

"She," corrected the salesman. "But you'll see that in a moment or two she'll relax."

The dog did. Maria petted the pup's soft fur. Paul absently touched the checkbook in his sports jacket pocket, then stood and told the salesman they'd have to think about it.

Outside the store a Salvation Army volunteer rang a silent bell and held up a sign that read RING, RING. Shoppers rushed about. Paul and Maria shared an Orange Julius. "It's a lot of money," Paul said.

"She's so adorable," Maria said, her dark hair spilling over the leather collar of her coat. "I can't stand to think of her having to spend Christmas in that damn window."

There was nothing they could do. By the time Bingo was two years old she'd had kennel cough, bronchitis, seizures, and finally allergies. Paul and Maria sat in the waiting rooms of veterinarians. There was little the vets could do except mark the dog's chart and cash Paul's checks. The last vet was named Alonzo Scarr, and at a red light on the way home Paul joked that clearly the man had never had a future as a plastic surgeon. Maria held Bingo in her arms. She didn't smile. "So of course he became a veterinarian," Paul said, forcing his joke, hoping to make Maria laugh, to break the tension. "I mean, with a last name like Scarr—"

Maria said nothing. The car behind them honked. The red

light had changed to green. Dr. Scarr had said with compas-
sion and utter seriousness that Bingo was allergic to nearly
everything.

This was after Maria and Paul had followed his advice and
put the dog on a cottage cheese and vegetable oil diet. Dr.
Scarr said, "Your dog has severe environmental allergies, and
I could check her for sixty agents but she'll show positive on
fifty-eight of them." Paul said, "Then she's allergic to life."
The vet scratched his head and nodded. By then Bingo was a
mass of scabs—an itching, bleeding mess of fur and nail, flesh
and tooth—and nothing, not even the bimonthly shots, could
heal her.

"It's a real racket," a professor in criminal justice told Paul
one afternoon in the department mailroom. "See, they breed
these poor animals in puppy mills in states where animal wel-
fare regulations are lax. The pups are neurotic and plagued
with genetic disorders common to their breed. The dogs are
literally bred to death. My neighbors made the same mistake.
Had to have the dog put down. Their kids really took it hard."

Maria was working the night shift at the library that semester. "We have to do something," she'd tell Paul when she
came home. She was just starting to show. She'd drink a glass
of juice and sigh, then rock Bingo in her arms and say she
wished she knew the answer. Paul watched television with the
dog that semester. Their favorite show was "All Creatures
Great and Small" on PBS. The set was new and Paul liked to
make the colors bright, giving Mr. Herriot's face a garish red-
ness. He talked to the dog when Maria wasn't home. "See,"
he'd say to Bingo, who'd squat beside him on the wooden
floor, incessantly scratching her chest and neck, "Tristan's got
himself in hot water with Siegfried again, but Mr. Herriot's
sure to save the day."

Dr. Scarr was silent as he filled the large hypodermic. Maria's small hands held Bingo's trembling face. Really, it was
the best thing; the dog couldn't even eat without scratching

herself. "Relax, honey," Maria said. The first of her tears splashed on the stainless steel table. Paul was at school, teaching his seminar. Something about stratification. His specialty was something about stratification. It was all too complex. They could try another vet, but they'd already been to three and now Bingo's skin was badly infected and it wasn't even flea season and in five months if everything went well they'd have the baby. Dr. Scarr stepped forward, then coughed. The night before, watching Bingo try to eat, Paul had announced, "I'm going to firebomb the pet store." "Is it the right thing?" Maria had asked. "You know, is it cruel to kill her?" Paul paced the length of the kitchen. "The only thing holding me back is knowing I'd have the blood of innocent goldfish on my hands." Bingo was licking her chops, then scratched open a fresh scab. "It's more cruel to let her live," Maria concluded. She stroked the dog's ears. Scarr withdrew the needle, and Bingo slumped. "Oh," Maria cried. He listened to the dog's sides with a stethoscope. Maria would tell Paul what she'd done that afternoon at lunch. A person shouldn't have to kill his first dog. "It's O.K.," Maria said to Bingo, her voice thick.

"She's passed," Dr. Scarr said, not looking at Maria.

In his dark brown corduroy sports jacket, khaki shirt, and tan corduroy pants, Paul teaches aggressively and well. His peer evaluations say he is dynamic. Dynamic is their euphemism for controversial. Paul's methods are the subject of many mailroom gossip sessions. He knows the hush that sometimes falls around the white alphabetized boxes when he enters the room means that the old men were discussing him. What should be done with the young assistant professor? The consensus leans toward granting him tenure; his colleagues feel it will settle him down. Paul thinks of his colleagues as "the old men." He thinks of most of them as brontosaurs waiting to sink into the mud and die. They're a turgid lot, going

through the same motions, reading the same yellowed lecture
notes semester after semester. They are predictable and therefore safe. Students tolerate them. Paul is erratic, daring. Students either love him or hate him. His troubles with the old
men and the higher administration began the day he threw the
portable desk.

He didn't throw the desk very far—actually, he only shoved
it—but the portable desk toppled and clattered and the noise
woke his dreaming students and rang out through the silent
halls. Paul shoved the desk for emphasis, to make a point, to
drive home an idea. There is nothing safe and predictable
about ideas, he believes. Sometimes ideas should strike you
with thunder. He wants to make thunder, to knock the compla-
cent off their high horse. He wants the exchange of ideas to
firebomb the world.

The Dean called Paul into his office. The Dean said he was
aware that any number of instructional techniques could, in the
proper circumstances, be viable, but the abuse of university
property was at best an unorthodox method that was untenable
and certainly was not to be encouraged by administrative per-
sonnel. The Dean smoked a large cigar while he spoke. Hundreds of ceramic and mahogany toads covered his bookshelves
and desk. The Dean had once been a biologist who led an
excursion into South America in the search for new sub-
families of toads. Some of the toads' backsides were covered
with bunches of ceramic eggs. On the Dean's desk was a
plaque that read BUFO AMERICANUS. Paul reassured the Dean
that his actions did not damage the desk. He said he chose an
especially sturdy-looking desk to shove, aware of the appropriate respect university employees should afford university
property. The Dean did not recognize Paul's sarcasm. Nev-
ertheless, Paul said, the instructional technique would not be
used by him again.

"Then we're eyeball to eyeball on this," the Dean said,
puffing on his cigar and standing and extending his hand.

"Yes," Paul said. "Thank you for your counsel."

Paul wasn't unlike his students when he first entered college. But the climate of campus life was different then. There was an undeclared war in Asia, riots in the cities' ghettos, angry women who wore buttons that read OFF OUR BACKS. There were people who argued about DDT and ecology. Paul read *Silent Spring, One-Dimensional Man, Soul on Ice, Sisterhood Is Powerful*. He listened to lunchtime debates in the boisterous Student Union. The ideas made a firestorm in his mind. When the National Guard invaded the campus, and students and professors went out on strike, and peaceful demonstrations were tear-gassed and scattered—legs tripped by nightsticks, heads and ribs clubbed—Paul felt a sudden spiritual manifestation, what he learned in Soph Lit was called an epiphany. He didn't have to be frightened. *He could matter.* So he became an active student radical. He helped coordinate teach-ins. He petitioned City Hall for permits to demonstrate, to march. He organized his thoughts. He felt he was a part of something and agreed with the student at Radcliffe who in 1968 said, "We do not feel like a cool, swinging generation— we are eaten up inside by an intensity that we cannot name." Paul read *The Guardian, Ramparts, Zap Comics, The Berkeley Tribe.* He was making decisions that would affect him for the rest of his life. He joined a group that put on guerrilla theater. He rapped with guardsmen, lent them magazines to read, brought them coffee from Dunkin Donuts. After he was arrested during a demonstration in his senior year, the university attempted to withhold his degree. There was a month of hearings about all those who'd been arrested. Paul read Isaac Deutscher's book on Trotsky's early life, *The Prophet Armed,* during much of the hearings. A lower court overruled the university's findings to expel. Paul was graduated in good standing.

He returned to the city and for two years worked in factories. Then he went to graduate school. He met Maria. They fell in love. He completed the work on his dissertation.

The old men crabbed about growing course loads and static pay scales. They swapped stories about how ignorant their students were. Stories about absurdly ignorant students earned the loudest mailroom laughs. When one old full professor retired, he mimeographed a booklet of quotes from his years' worst student essays. Paul didn't find it funny. "If they're so damn dumb," he told the laughing old men, "why in hell don't you teach them?" The retiring professor scratched the side of his grotesquely large bald head. "That's why we hired you, you naive fool. Waste all your juice on the comatose shits. Gentlemen, I'm going fishing."

Paul wears the story like a badge. He tells it whenever the untenured faculty gathers to complain. The young assistants nod, sip white wine or Lite beer, repeat their stories, shake their heads.

Yet Paul cannot really empathize with his students. They seem to him to be hedonistic, concerned mainly with copping highs and getting laid. Today's students are into escapism, he tells the young assistants. Their primary contribution to American society has been to make "party" into a verb. Where SEIZE THE TIME used to be written, now was scrawled PARTY DOWN. The students seem too close to the old men, Paul thinks. It's as if the students realized that the smorgasbord of good times was running out, but instead of working and struggling to replenish the tables they jostled only to load up their empty plates before it was too late. At his most cynical, Paul confesses to Maria that what the students need is a good taste of repression. The spur to the side of the sleeping horse. Then he immediately says, "No, I don't really mean that. Listen to me, I'm talking crazy. I must be getting old."

Maria was in junior high when Paul experienced his epiphany. World events bore her, though on principle she is against all forms of violence and war. She is glad she came of age when she did. She has an active imagination. She doesn't need to experience directly the burning pain of pepper gas to know

it makes you sneeze and choke. Government plays for keeps,
Maria believes. Authority is brutal because brutality is en-
demic to authority. Maria doesn't like pain. She is wary of
dentists, always polite to policemen. The major issues when
she was in school were dress codes and whether the seniors
could have a smoking lounge. Her ninth-grade class helped put
together a rally for peace in the school auditorium; Maria neatly
lettered a rainbow sign that read WORLD PEACE—LET'S TRY IT!
She was attentive in class and did most of her homework, and
each afternoon, after riding in a girlfriend's mother's car to a
girlfriend's house where the girls sipped Tab and talked about
clothes and boys and new records, she got high. Maria is an
expert smoker of grass. She can smoke a joint down so close to
her lips it resembles a half-moon sliver of fingernail, and that's
not even using a roach clip. On the weekends she worked in a
department store, selling mascara and lip gloss and cologne to
large, overdressed women who already used too much perfume and makeup. Maria seldom uses makeup. She is naturally pretty, with good cheekbones, her eyelashes naturally
thick. When Paul met her at a party after a Grateful Dead
concert, she smelled like Ivory soap and marijuana smoke.

Demonstrations frighten her, as do most overt displays of
emotion. Why can't people be civilized and just talk things
out? Maria thinks. War belongs to another world, like boxing.
She cannot see any sense in people hitting each other, even if
they're being paid millions of dollars to do it. It's stupid, she
thinks, and the people who watch it and cheer are stupider, and
in most arguments she leaves the room or concedes. "You're
absolutely correct," she agrees. But of course she isn't con-
vinced; her surrender is only a ploy that helps her get past the
time when someone else wants to argue. She knows that Paul
finds her behavior irritating, but that is his problem. Maria
loves Paul because of it, because he is what she isn't. Yin and
yang. Though she tells him to change, to see life as more than
mere sets of social and political theories, she realizes that his

personality is set as granite. If she were a nation she'd be Switzerland. Neutral. Protected by snowcapped mountains. Maker of watches, peace talks, chocolate. No taste fills the mouth as darkly, as completely, as chocolate. When Maria studied European geography in tenth grade she turned in so many extra-credit reports on Switzerland that her teacher raised the white flag and gave her a 101 on her report card. In college she received a degree in library science. She is very serious about libraries. She finds them civil, even better than churches because in libraries you can move about. Everything has its place in a library. The Dewey Decimal System was as great an advancement as the discovery of the wheel. Everyone is equal in a library, and everyone knows it is improper to raise your voice. Whenever there's any unnecessary noise, all a librarian has to do is say, "Shhh." People are usually grateful when you help them find a book.

The sole imperfection, Maria thinks, is the copying room. There the coin exchangers clank; the Xerox machines groan and whir. The copiers break the spines of books. The area is somehow impure, as sacrilegious as a Coca-Cola machine in a cathedral.

Maria is fond of sitting on a ladder in the graduate stacks, surrounded by books, reading. The gentle hum of the building's ventilation system is the only sound she hears. She imagines that she is the keeper of ideas, the custodian of civilization, and outside the walls of her fortress the barbarians wage war against the vandals, but the library walls keep her safe. All of the explosive issues rest quietly on their shelves. Sometimes Maria thinks of herself as a monk, sheltering the written word, in the darkest days of the Dark Ages. Except for celibacy, she might have liked the life of a nun. She is often overwhelmed by the brash cacophony of life. In traffic jams, when others around her impatiently inch forward and blow their horns, she shifts into neutral and slowly idles, concentrating on the stutter of *r*'s her engine continues to pronounce. Sometimes she smokes a joint in the library's third-floor ladies room. Marijuana pacifies her. Good marijuana puts a warm coat of varnish on her eyes. Then she is glazed, safe, protected by the haze the reefer gives her; the flow of life's madness is slowed down, and she can cope.

Maria accepts her Hispanic roots matter of factly, and she thinks that in a past life she once was Swiss. Though she claims she doesn't believe in organized religion, she wears a gold crucifix on a chain around her neck and makes the sign of the Cross whenever she hears an ambulance. Maria believes in tarot cards, palm readings, astrology, the interpretation of dreams. Death always comes in threes and always knocks on the door or wall. One morning when she was sixteen she was brushing her hair, getting ready for school, when her grandmother rushed in to ask if she had heard the knocks. That afternoon her grandmother died. Then an uncle died, then Maria's cousin. Maria is proud of the story. When Paul hears her repeat it and criticizes her for not being rational, she says, "Paul, you're so limited I could laugh."

Maria is very aware of how tentative human life on the planet is. Secure on her ladder in the graduate stacks, she reads the predictions of Nostradamus. She studies the teachings of Edgar Cayce. She believes in good and evil, and she knows she has had many past lives. In at least one of them she knew Paul; that is why he seems so comfortable to be around. Their unconsciousnesses recognize each other. Maria can't remember any details of her past lives. The fact that she has lived before is enough.

People are born, she believes, and they live and do good and evil. Then they're born again and again and again, until they do mostly good. Until they don't have to work through anything anymore. She knows she has many more lives to live.

She believes the body growing in her womb is just that, a body. It will become complete later, when a soul floating in the cosmos selects it. When a soul chooses her and Paul. So she and Paul need to be very good because many souls are judging them. Paul needs to fight against some of his rigidity. She needs more backbone, more courage to stand up, to define. She knows that this spring is a very special time, tentative as an interview. But if Nostradamus is correct, the world will end during the child's lifetime. This worries Maria.

Sometimes she sits by herself late at night, arms around herself, rocking, weeping. She weeps for the future her child will see. What a bitter world, she thinks. What an obscene, violent, horrible mess. Don't come down to us if you're frightened, she tells the souls in the cosmos. We have very little to offer, so wouldn't it be better if you wait? If none of the souls choose to come down, Maria prays to God, let me miscarry. I'm not forcing you, she tells the soul of her baby. Choose me and Paul, if we are what you need. Come to us—we welcome you—even though I know your death will break my heart when the world ends, when the ground is shaken by earthquakes, when the end comes and death falls like a rain of hailstones from the broken sky.

So Paul and Maria watch the evening news because it seldom fails to reaffirm their separate beliefs. Paul turns up the volume, adjusts the color, then settles on the couch. The best minds of the sixties had foreseen all of this, he thinks. But being right gives him little solace. He hopes the world can resolve its problems. He is tired and wants to grow old in relative stability and peace. Is that too much to ask for? he thinks. He knows the answer. Of course it's too much, because he and the rest of America are still so damn privileged, and because order naturally deteriorates into chaos and chaos makes fertile ground for discontent, insurrection, and war. The next war will be with nuclear weapons, he believes. Has man ever made a tool he didn't use eventually? It's the bottom of the ninth inning, he thinks, and there are no runners on base; the good guys are ten thousand runs behind, and the final pitch is on its way. Soon it will explode in the catcher's over-sized mitt, and somebody will fire a nuclear warhead, and in a cloud of fire the world as we know it will be gone.

Even schoolchildren can recite the scenario, Paul thinks. No wonder they smoke angel dust and impregnate one another by the time they are thirteen. *Carpe diem.* He knows it is insane. It is insane to sit in the faculty dining room of the student cafeteria and actually discuss with the young assistants how the world will end. His theory is that the planet itself will remain intact after the bombs are unleashed, but mammals, reptiles, birds, and most of the fish will be destroyed; plant life will be devastated, but some insects will survive, and some fish, so deep in the oceans that they continue to defy discovery. These forms of life will be left. So it will not really be the end of the world, Paul argues. Only the end of *us.* Then the analogy is humanity as dinosaur—human as extinct, lumbering beast. Our skeletons will adorn the insect museums of the future, he jokes, and future praying mantis larvae will ask their mothers what happened to the mammals, the reptiles, the birds, the large fish. Mommy, why did they become extinct? Oh, the wise praying mantis mother will say, we have any number of theories. They might have been destroyed by a supernova. Maybe large meteors fell from the sky and raised so much dust it erased the sun. Perhaps they burned too much fossil fuel and as a result of the greenhouse effect the polar icecaps melted. Some think man learned nuclear fission, but that's an extreme viewpoint. Even the ignorant aphids know not to experiment with *that.*

The ground ball skips back to the pitcher. He picks it up easily and scoops it underhand to first. Out. The ball game's over.

Maria leaves the room now that the news is on. She leaves, but cannot help but listen. "Paul," she says, "do you have to watch it?"

"What would you rather I do?" he says. "Shut my eyes?
Turn on 'The Beverly Hillbillies'?"

"Anything," Maria says, pouring a glass of valpolicella in
the kitchen. She touches her growing abdomen, is aware of the
fullness of her breasts. Everything makes her think of the fate
of her coming baby. The face of the Argentine widow staring
grimly at the flag-draped coffin. The Irish children throwing
back canisters of tear gas in the Ulster streets. Women wearing
babushkas in food lines in Poland. The crack of automatic ri-
fles in El Salvador. The very worst are the pictures of the
starving children in Africa. Arms like wooden spoons, dis-
tended stomachs, flies crawling on their nostrils and open lips.
Why can't the news limit itself to the weather? she thinks.
Cars abandoned in ragged rows on a highway after a blizzard,
homes that shouldn't have been built on mountainsides in the
first place sliding down a lake of mud. These are the things
Maria can watch, can understand. Hurricanes. Floods. A
tragic fire. Children playing with matches. Her baby will never
play with matches. Already she has started to childproof the
house.

Can the world be childproofed for her and Paul? she wonders.

They always end the evening news with a light note, a hu-
morous touch. Exit laughing. A story about the grandmother
in Florida who opened her house trailer to hundreds of foster
children over the past thirty years—"There Was an Old
Woman Who Lived in a Shoe." The Oklahoma cowboy who
lived in a cage full of rattlesnakes for several months but who
now wouldn't be listed in *The Guinness Book of World Records*. Pathos and irony. In Virginia Beach a man hacked his
mother-in-law to death with a hatchet and claimed as his de-
fense that he thought she was a raccoon.

Absurd. A commercial for something called Intellivision
begins, and a shill praises it over other video-game systems

because only Intellivision offers the total destruction of a planet. So their gravest fear is now a feature on a video game? The glass of red wine falls from Maria's hand. It shatters on the linoleum like a destructing planet. Paul rushes into the kitchen. And that's the way it is—

Later that evening, the television off, Paul sits on the couch with Maria. Her head rests against his chest. His arm hangs over her shoulder. They have sat like this since the room began to darken. Neither has wanted to disturb the other, to get up and turn on a light. The open window next to the sofa flutters the thin curtains that hang over it. From the even way he is breathing, Maria thinks Paul is asleep.

"Are you sleeping?" she whispers.

Paul's breathing stops, then starts again. "No."

"You never told me why you came home early today."

He lets out a long breath. "My three o'clock didn't read the assignment, so I told them to go to the registrar and withdraw from school."

"Why?" Maria asks.

"Sometimes the best way to get people's attention is to exaggerate."

Maria thinks about exaggeration. Then she swallows. "I can't tell you how much I want to get high."

"Let me give you a backrub."

"I don't want a backrub."

"Have a glass of wine."

"I'm sick of wine."

"I'm sorry." Paul doesn't know what else to say.

Her hand clutches his arm. The strength surprises him. "Are you sure having the baby is the right thing?"

"Yes," Paul says, too quickly. He isn't sure.

"I wouldn't do this for anyone else, you know."

"I know." His hand pats her hand. "It's the right thing,

Maria." The hand squeezes her wrist. "Everything will be O.K."

She turns her head, trying in the darkness to look at him, but she can't see any of the features of his face. She can only hear his even, reassuring voice as he begins to explain that even though an event seems likely it is never guaranteed to happen, that it's useless to walk through life feeling depressed and powerless, that the birth of a baby is an affirmation, an act of great courage, faith, and hope. For all we know, Paul continues, when things look their very bleakest we'll be visited by spaceships from a distant galaxy, and the alien life forms will help us solve all our problems. Maria scoffs at the idea, though it's tempting to believe. Paul softly laughs and says it comes from a movie, a classic, *The Night of the Living Dead.* Maria doesn't laugh at the joke. No, Paul says, it was *The Day the Earth Stood Still,* the best science-fiction movie ever made. Maria says she wishes the earth *would* stand still. It can't, Paul says, suddenly serious. He tries to think of something else to say.

"Sometimes when I come down here in the morning I still expect to see Bingo," Maria says. Paul's eyes dart in the darkness, looking for the dog. Maria sits up and faces him. She places her hands in his. "Why did she have to die?"

Paul feels on safer ground now. He knows the answer to the question. "Free enterprise. We were ripped off. We were suckered. We live in a country where salesmen can dress up like doctors and lovable little puppy dogs can grow up allergic to life."

"And we're not?" Maria says.

Paul reaches for all the hopefulness he has to offer. "No," he says. "Maria, we're the luckiest people in the world. Look at us. We're both alive and healthy. Our baby's on its way. We have a house, work, food. Ninety-five percent of the world would give their arms and legs to have half of what we have."

Paul's voice is high, speedy. "And maybe our baby will be the one who helps solve the world's problems. Maybe not. But if the child ever asks me why we agreed for it to be born—" He hesitates. His eyes search the darkness for the answer. "I'll say I thought having a chance to live was better than no chance, even if we live to see the world destroyed."

Maria laughs, terrified. "I can just see it. The bombs will be falling down around our heads and you'll be explaining all of that to our baby."

"I'll be digging a hole, Maria. I'll wear the colander on my head. You and the baby bring the cans of beans. We'll do what we can to survive."

"I'll just stand in the backyard and hold my baby and weep."

"No, you won't." Paul shakes her shoulders. "We'll struggle. We're not cynics. We'll march in the streets. We'll influence opinion. We'll do what we must to survive." He takes her in his arms and holds her tightly.

Maria feels his arms around her and relaxes, thinking about her coming baby. Choose us, she prays, because we're not cynics. Choose us because Paul is so stubborn. Because I'll hold you to my breast until I die. The idea of holding her child gives her comfort, and Maria imagines that at this moment a very special and wise and trusting soul chooses the body floating in the warm waters of her womb. She believes she can feel the soul as it enters her body. Yes. The child within her stirs. Tears of wonder fall from her eyes.

Paul feels Maria's tears and thinks she is despairing. "Please," he says. "Let's not think anymore. Maria, please."

She cries freely now, rejoicing.

Paul goes on thinking. He gives full play to his doubts. Maybe this *is* the very worst moment to be alive, especially in America, the eye of the dragon, belly of the beast. Maybe this *is* the absolutely worst moment to have the audacity to give

birth to an innocent. Maria's shoulders shake with what Paul
thinks is great sadness. He stares past her at the television squatting smugly in the
corner of the room. Before the end comes, he thinks, everyone
will see it, in living color, splashed across a hundred million
TV screens. The multicolored maps, areas of greatest risk,
perhaps even the warheads' trajectories. Certainly the as-
surance that the war is winnable. Certainly the glib warnings
to stay calm. Maria is filled with joy. I'll make the colors so
intense they'll blind me, he thinks. I'll turn up the volume
until I grow deaf. He squeezes Maria so fiercely that she
makes a squeak. Then I'll open all the windows, and I'll throw
open the front door, and I'll turn on the water in the bathroom
and the kitchen, and I'll flick on every light, turn on the stereo,
the oven, the furnace, the air conditioner— Then I'll wait in
the backyard with Maria, with our baby. Paul's nightmare
stops. His hand reaches down and touches the swelling round-
ness of Maria's belly. She is soft and warm, happy, in his
arms. He feels the darkest despair he has ever known.

The curtains over the open window next to them billow suddenly like an enormous cloud.

My Father's Laugh

My name is Thaddeus Alexander Cooper III, but you can call me Thaddeus. I'm sitting here in Marsha's bedroom looking out the window and writing this, and I'm wondering when it's going to rain. I know that it will rain. That and the fact that I'm writing this to save my goddamn life are the only two things I'm certain of. So try to hear me out. And realize, as well, that I plan to milk this. For all that I can get. You've been warned. As my father, may his dear dead soul rest forever in peace, always used to say, "Move away from the window, lady, can't you see I'm driving?" I ask that you give me room.

My mother once told me, "Thaddeus, someday you're going to meet someone who's just a little bit bigger than you are and he's going to kick in your ass." She'd wave her big spoon at me and wipe her hands on her apron when she'd say that. Now that I think, she's told me that countless times.

But neither my father nor my mother, nor my Uncle Karl, nor Marsha, for that matter, has anything to do with this story. This story will be about the rain. You should know that my father is no longer with us; he pulled the cord and got off this bus blocks ago. That my mother is a maker of soup. I dislike soup. That my uncle is my uncle. That Marsha is a writer. These are the facts.

I'll tell you this: this is lie. You be my judge. I'm writing this to get into Marsha's underpants. That's the truth, my reader.

Marsha is the kind of girl who likes—how shall I put it? Marsha likes the kind of boy who does things with seriousness, with direction, as she puts it, adding that the world already has more than its share of buffoons like me. Obviously, I disagree. Thaddeus Alexander Cooper III is no buffoon, and if you'd like to compare philosophies, Horatio, I'll tell you now that mine is the one that best enables me to survive. That's what it's all about, isn't it? I pound these drab green dormitory walls and argue; I make suggestive comments and pray that Marsha will understand. I quote to her the wisdom of my father: "If you wanted to be let off in front of your house, my pretty, why the hell didn't you take a taxi?" I hope you, reader, can catch my drift. "I'm not here delivering pizzas," I tell her. "Marsha, you'll get only what I have to give."

Which isn't pizza, seriousness, or direction, though I do badly want to direct something between her legs. I know what I know; I have what I need. I am the son of my father, the son of a bus driver, the son of fixed routes and scheduled stops. I have what I need.

With the exception of the story that will save me. That my dead father failed to leave me, and I've looked for it in soup bowls and not found it. My uncle offers me only the back of his hand. And Marsha? Marsha claims to be saving herself.

"For what?" I ask.

She shrugs. Her nipples brush against her blouse as she does this.

"The world could end tomorrow," I tell her.

She shakes her silly head.

And I shake mine. These students, you realize, haven't yet learned how to live. Sometimes they make me feel like a wolf in their midst. I'm not a student, you see. I attend no classes. I pay no tuition. I don't have an I.D.

Though you've seen me around. I'm the guy who holds up the line trying to explain how I left my I.D. in my other pants. I'm the guy who sits in the frantic cafeteria during finals week sipping water and doing double acrostics. I'm the guy leaning against the tree on the first day of spring. I smile. I nod. I wink as you walk by.

You too shake your head.

But Marsha didn't the night I met her, though I can't be entirely certain since it happened over the phone. I have a friend named Stuart who has a friend named Jo who was Marsha's roommate until very recently, and I first heard from them that Marsha was a wonderful and beautiful girl.

"Introduce me," I said.

They said they would but didn't. I realized they were a dead-end street. So I put my proverbial noodle in the sauce pan and waited one fine evening for Jo to leave the dormitory. Then I sauntered to the corner pay phone.

"Hello," I said, "is Jo there?"

Marsha said no and asked if there was a message. I liked her voice and carefully explained that I had an exam the following day and was calling to see if Jo could take me to the dormitory library. Admission required a resident I.D. Marsha repeated that Jo was out. I thanked her for the information. Then Marsha sighed and offered to take me to the library herself.

"No," I said. "That would be too much to ask of a stranger."

"Well, it isn't exactly like we're strangers," Marsha said. "We're both friends of Jo. Do you have a name? My name is Marsha."

"My name is Thaddeus Alexander Cooper III, but you can call me Thaddeus."

"Hello, Thaddeus."

"Hello, Marsha."

"I can meet you down in the lobby in ten minutes if you'd like."

I said sure, then checked the coin return. At the dormitory I waited in the lounge. When a wonderful and beautiful girl appeared, looking about through a pair of thick-lensed glasses, I approached her and took her hand. She said, "Thaddeus?" "In the flesh," I said. I flashed her my best smile. We walked upstairs. I watched her shapely legs take the steps two at a time. Outside the library she turned suddenly and said, "Thaddeus, where are your books?" I struck my forehead. "Where is my mind?" She laughed, and as I took her arm I suggested we go to the snack bar instead for some coffee.

There Marsha told me she wanted to be a writer and that she would like her writing to change the world and make it a better place in which to have children. I told her I was a disgruntled economics major. I closely watched her face. I said economics was very mercenary. Then I hung my head and lowered my voice and confessed to be looking for something meaningful to do with my life. I think that was the clincher, the word "meaningful." After I said it, Marsha sipped her tea with lemon and beamed.

My reader, I am well aware that you sit somewhere wondering what will happen to Thaddeus when Marsha discovers what kind of fellow he really is. He is a rogue, you think. A manipulator, a liar, perhaps even a jerk. There he sits writing in her dormitory bedroom; he has designs on her hymen; he openly admits his deceit. Like my mother and my uncle you frown upon me, but understand my hand. Marsha knows that I'm not an economics major nor a student nor entirely honest, but since I have told her these things myself she has come to respect me. Reread that. Marsha respects, even admires, my *honesty* about my dishonesty. She says that is a start. To her I am a challenge. These lies are the basis of our relationship.

You're sitting here before me very quietly. Your eyes are open, so you must not be asleep. Do you have any questions? Am I making everything clear? I invite any and all questions. Just raise your hand and shout out.

A dark woman in the back row asks what I look like.

A fine question, miss. As you can see, I'm thin and youthful, fond of wearing black, and also extremely handsome, in a sensitive, tubercular, swashbuckling sort of way. Yes, the group kneeling in the aisle.

I beg your pardon.

No, Sisters, this isn't a lecture on *Hamlet.*

Who sold them tickets?

A voluptuous young thing in a bikini asks what I do in my spare time.

Miss, allow me a moment to think. I do so much, you realize. I ski and ride horses and scuba dive; I play rugby, baccarat, jai alai, mah-jongg, and ice hockey. I'm an avid reader of the classics, and I keep a macaw and several salt-water turtles in my home. I'm a lifetime subscriber to *National Geographic,* and I shoot big game whenever and wherever I can.

The redhead tonguing the banana.

"Thaddeus, why do you write?"

My pet, I'll quote for you my father. He said, "If you wanted a seat by the window, halfback, how come you're standing here next to me in the aisle?" By this he meant that if you want something done you should do it yourself. My dear, and all of you millions of readers and listeners out there, I feel that in these times of economic strife and spiritual uneasiness there is a crying need for literature which will help lead us out of the wilderness and onto the paths that will make this world a decent place in which to have children. So I'm merely trying to do my bit, to carry my share of the load, and I hope, yes I sincerely do hope, that if each and every one of you who hears my voice could do just one nice thing today, then this old world will soon be a great place in which to have children.

I trust you now recognize the extent of my integrity. Marsha, as you know, already has.

"We've got to communicate," I told her one evening.

She asked me what I meant.

"Well, Marsha," I began, "we mean so much to me."
"Yes," she said.
"But we've been living a lie, Marsha," I blurted.
Then I sat her down and told her everything: how I am not a student, how I do not have a lakeside apartment but really live with my mother in the back of the tiny restaurant, how I do not have a job programming computers for the Coast Guard, how I have had to put up with the back of my uncle's hand after my father died, how I am not a connoisseur of gourmet foods but have eaten my mother's soup for more than half my life and still intensely dislike it. I hid my face as I spoke these words. I wrung my hands. I tried to gnash my teeth. Then I said: "Marsha, after all of this, surely you cannot like me anymore."

She began crying. I moved slowly toward her, comforting her, taking off her Coke-bottle glasses, brushing my hands against her breasts.

"Thaddeus," she said, "you can't really mean that."
"Oh," I said, "but I do."
"But you're wrong," she said, smiling. "I still like you. In fact, I like you even more now that you've told me the truth."
"You cannot be serious," I said.
"Thaddeus, I am. Don't you realize that it took far greater courage for you to have told me these things, and that you must be even more of a good and meaningful person to have been able to say them?"
"Don't compliment me," I said sternly. "You deserve better than me."
"Oh no, Thaddeus. No, no."

I had her blouse off and was working on the zipper of her jeans when Jo had to come in with Stuart, which was fine with me. Let's pretend we're not here, Marsha, I whispered, but she quickly dressed and led me into the front room, saying hey everybody, let's have a party, and I had an awful time.

For weeks after that she pleaded with me to take her to my

mother's tiny restaurant. I finally consented, but I insisted we go in disguise. I told her it was better to test the waters before leaping. Marsha agreed that my idea had good intentions, but outside the restaurant she tore off my rubber eyeglasses with attached false nose and furry mustache and pushed me inside the door. As I picked myself up from the restaurant floor I shrugged and called out, "Guess who I brought home for soup, darling Mother?"

Marsha liked my mother very much. She told me later that she could really empathize with the trauma of being a blue-collar woman living without the support of her husband and having no one, really, to lean on. I told her my mother leans on my uncle. I told her my uncle leans heavily on me. I told her the colors of collars have little to do with anything, that what is important is the bulge in the back pocket. I quoted to her the wisdom of my father: "Sorry, sweetheart, I can't change anything over a five."

My mother fed Marsha more than soup. She ladled out the assessment that her son was a bum; then she peppered Marsha's impressionable young mind with the idea that she could reform me. It was a challenge of sorts. Marsha chewed on it slowly, then swallowed and smiled, the stupid zeal of newfound direction shining from her eyes upon me like twin headlights.

She was so excited that evening that when we returned to her dormitory she turned to me and unbuttoned the top two buttons of her blouse. She smiled and asked me if I didn't feel a little overdressed. I told her I felt fine. Marsha removed her blouse, then dropped the straps of her bra down over her shoulders and asked if I could give her a backrub. I told her I didn't think it was her back she wanted rubbed. She giggled and unhooked her bra.

"No, Thaddeus. Not my back."

I was standing in her closet. Marsha approached, rotating her hips, her thumbs hooked in the belt loops of her jeans. I got a sudden headache. My stomach knotted. I started to wheeze and sneeze. Marsha toyed with the tongue on her zipper, flicking it first up, then a notch at a time down. I could smell mothballs. My eyes were watering. Calmly Marsha stepped from her jeans.

"It's getting late," I said.

"But, Thaddeus. The night's just started."

"Really," I said, "I have to go." My reader, as you can figure, it was the evening's soup that sickened me; my tongue felt thick in my mouth and my vision was all in a blur. Still Marsha stalked me, chasing me out of the closet and into the front room. I felt like a rat in a trap. I scurried back to the bedroom, attempting to hide beneath the bed; then I ran into the tiny kitchen where I leaned back against the refrigerator and feigned passing out. Marsha opened the cupboard in search of a glass for water. Terrified, I bolted past her and out the door of the dorm apartment, making at last my escape.

I'm out of breath. Yes, I see there are more questions. Just call out.

"Mr. Cooper, er, Thaddeus, could you tell us what is your favorite part of the story?" asks a feathered woman holding a bow and arrow.

Yes, miss. I smile. Your question.

Aren't I the charmer?

"Thaddeus, do you have any peculiar writing habits?" asks an elderly woman with pencils sticking out from her hair.

I'm very glad you asked me that question, ma'am. I have to admit that like most writers I like a clean and comfortable work area, preferably a bedroom with a window in a dormitory, and that I like to write under the constant expectation that at any given moment the door will fly open and Marsha will leap into my arms, proud and happy of this, the story that will save me.

The old woman with the tattered coat and matching shopping bags?

"I'm your mother."

Hello, Ma.

"This is a dirty story."

No it isn't, Ma.

"Thaddeus, don't tell *me*. I know dirt when I see it."

Hey, not in front of all these people, Ma.

"You raise a kid in a decent home and feed his face three times a day and look at what he does for you: he writes pornography."

As my father—your husband—always used to say, "If you ain't got a quarter or a token there, grandma, you and your purse can get off at the next stop."

And presently I too am approaching my stop. As I sit here, waiting for Marsha, staring out this dormitory window. The sky is gray and clouded. I want sun. Do you hear me up there? Sun?

I could write *The sun is shining* and you would think it was. But the sun isn't shining. And my writing it wouldn't make it so. I think I'm beginning to understand that.

It will rain. I hate the rain. If it weren't for the rain—

Oh well.

Has my life been saved? How about it, Marsha?

She doesn't seem to be able to come to the phone right now, my dear reader, so we'll just have to wait until next time to find out. Let me say, however, that it's been real. Remember, you knew me when.

We'll close with more words from my father.

"Put the corks back in your bottles, cowboys, this is the end of the line."

You take care now.

Sincerely,

Thaddeus Alexander Cooper III

I have been waiting here for four hours now. For a while I thumbed through a copy of *Cosmopolitan,* reading an interesting article about how to prepare cucumber bisque. Then for a while I lay down. I sat up. I turned the light off and on, oh, I'd say fifty or so times. The switch was stunning. Then I paced the room. There are six big steps the long way and four-and-a-half big steps the short way. This does not count the bedroom. Counting the bedroom, there are six more steps. There are two desks. Two chairs. Two beds. Two desk lamps. Two dressers. A pair of bulletin boards. I feel like I'm inside Noah's ark.

Yet there is only one window. This fact depresses me. If there were two windows, perhaps the second would offer me a different view. I am speaking figuratively. There *are* two windows, one in the front room and one here in the bedroom. But their vistas are identical.

I touched each at least one hundred times. I thought that by doing this I might change something. Six big steps, touch; six big steps, turn; six big steps, the same view. The only thing that changed was me. I got very tired. I sat down then and inspected the walls.

They seem made of cardboard. The exception is a small area above the bedroom window, which seems made of something else. It is brown. It's also circular, very much like a cloud, but unlike a cloud it doesn't remind me of anything except perhaps a water stain, or perhaps a cloud. I'm sitting directly beneath it right now.

On the front room walls are three pictures. The first has a young child running naked through a forest, looking as if someone or something is chasing it. In the treetops it reads TODAY IS THE FIRST DAY OF THE REST OF YOUR LIFE. So was yesterday. I cannot tell if the child is a girl or a boy.

The second is a print of a very uncomfortable-looking blue old man who is strumming an equally uncomfortable-looking blue guitar. A larger canvas might have made the two more comfortable. I didn't like this picture.

The third finds W. C. Fields squinting at a fistful of playing cards. Once I saw the movie this picture came from, and, as I remember, Fields was cheating. I cannot remember if he was caught.

Marsha has an interesting arrangement of books on her bookshelves. She separates fiction from nonfiction, as do most libraries, but Marsha does so artistically, with élan, with empty wine bottles and rocks and little clay pots filled with paper flowers. She also alphabetizes the books by authors, but then she places the books on her shelves according to height, with the tallest coming first. Fiction begins with *Don Quixote.* It is followed by *The Complete Works of Shakespeare, Tristram Shandy, Finnegans Wake,* and then the dictionary. Nonfiction begins with *The Divided Self* and ends with *I'm O.K., You're O.K.* I did not agree. The shelves looked so smug and pleased with themselves that for a good half hour I found myself compelled to rearrange them, hiding a few books beneath the couch and chairs and in the kitchen and bathroom, and dropping several of the rocks out the window onto the roofs of parked cars.

Then I indulged myself with one of my favorite and most profitable pastimes, sofa exploration. As I child I practiced this regularly in the restaurant, though there we had booths. The object of this activity is to make your hand as flat an instrument as is possible and then to insert it carefully into the crevices beneath the cushions, pulling out and keeping whatever items you may find. I found the following:

Two packs of matches. Both were from my mother's restaurant, Sarah Cooper's Kitchen. Their flaps read Homestyle Cuisine, A Neighborhood Place, Bring the Whole Family, Grandpa and Grandma Too, You'll Love Us.

Eighteen bobby pins. Thirteen were brown (Marsha's) and five were a kind of soupy yellow (Jo's). I did not like touching them.

Two pencils. The first was a newly sharpened yellow Number 2, from the university, NORTHWESTERN, with an abused eraser and a rather chewed back end. As I pulled it from the sofa I felt like I was stumbling onto something private; I imagined Marsha sitting there on the couch scratching out a story with it, or at least trying to, thinking, chewing the pencil's end, then erasing. I suppose, since the pencil is fairly long and the point is still sharp, that she didn't get very far with her initial conception. I put it back, along with the eighteen bobby pins.

The other pencil brought back a flood of unpleasant childhood memories, for either Marsha or Jo went to the same doctor I did. It is a very bright and colorful pencil, saying—allow me a moment to look—FROM YOUR DENTIST, FOR BEING A GOOD PATIENT.

And it has a great many balloons on it, and four clown faces. I'm using it right now. I'd type, but my fingers are exhausted.

In addition:

Thirty-eight cents. I've appropriated it as partial reparation for the gross inconvenience of waiting. Of the coins, by far the most unusual is a 1943 LIBERTY In God We Indeed Do Trust dime. It's a Lady-with-the-wings-coming-out-from-the-sides-of-her-head dime, and it frightened me because the tails side is—believe me now—blank. Are you listening?

When I first pulled it out, I thought it was a slug. Then I felt the ridges on its side, and upon flipping it over was most amazed to see the Lady. My question to you is this: how did the blank side become blank?

Is this dime one of those rare mistakes? If so, how many millions is it worth? Or is this counterfeit, the forgers having only enough time to imprint the one side? Or did somebody simply fuck it up? Excuse me, Sisters. Though I suspect that nobody is listening anyway. Hello, hello.

My question: is this true or is this false? I'll have to ask Marsha when she gets here. She'll know. Yes, Marsha will know. Though she might doubt that I wrote this. She just might say: "Thaddeus, just where did this come from?"

"Whatdya mean, where did this come from?" I'll say. "It's mine."

"All of this, Thaddeus? All of this is yours?"

"Sure." I feel very small. "Who do you think all this belongs to?"

"Thaddeus. Come in here for a moment." She is calling. I feel even smaller. "Thaddeus? Do you hear me? Thaddeus?"

"It's mine," I say again.

"Where's the fire, Sarah?" my father says.

"Look. Here in your son's closet. And here in his dresser drawer."

"Holy Moses, now there's something."

"It can't be all his. Ask him where he got it."

"Where'd you get this, Thaddeus?"

"Tha-dde-us?"

"Look here, Sarah. In his jacket pockets too."

"Where'd he go to? Thaddeus?"

"And look here in his Sunday shoes."

"Tha-dde-us?"

"Oh, gracious me, looky here. Tokens. So that's why I've been short."

"Thaddeus!"

"And dimes even here in the cuffs of his pants."

"Now where'd he go to?"

His cuffs were full too, I remember. I remember him coming home sitting in his big red chair next to the radio, and smiling and shining. His chest was shining, his number was 17381, and the stripes down the sides of his pants shone too, like they'd been polished, like the seat of his pants. He was a thin man, and he always had a smile and a rub on the head for his big boy. His cuffs, she would kneel before him and turn them out as he sipped his cup of coffee, and sipped, blew, his face red and his mustache laughing. She'd turn out his cuffs and he'd say looky at all those tonight, oh my, circles of paper, from his transfer punch. I would gather them, fill my two hands, save them in my dresser drawer, the bottom one, with all my coins, and in my closet a handful of each every day. I wanted to be like him. And at night sometimes I'd get behind him in his big red chair, the radio talking or singing, sometimes she sewing or writing on paper, or clucking her tongue at the table writing out bills, with paper, my fists full of paper, sneaking behind him, he sleeping, his head nodding, down on his newspaper, his tired glasses fallen to the end of his nose. Confetti, I'd cry. Wheeeee.

He'd jump, laugh his big laugh, pick up his big boy and kiss me.

Transfer confetti, wheeeee, a sip of his coffee, some horseyback.

"Thaddeus!"

"Thaddeus, your mother's calling you, Thaddeus."

"You take care of this. He's your duty this time."

"But, Sarah—"

"He respects you. Now where'd he go?"

"He probably doesn't even know that what he's been doing is—"

"Doesn't know?"

"He's a little fella, Sarah, he—"

"He has to be punished. He has to learn. Thaddeus!"

"Thaddeus!"

"Thaddeus, this is so good I can't believe you wrote it."

"All by myself, Marsha."

"How long did it take you?"

"Oh, only a couple of hours—"

A couple of beers, no more, dead, the cans even warm now, must take a look, I'll be back

in a second, and you didn't even notice I had gone. The kitchen is one-and-a-half small steps the short way, and three big steps the long, assuming I could walk through the refrigerator, which I did, looking in the back by the coils where Stuart, ha ha ha, had hidden a bottle; so make yourself comfortable, my dear reader, we're in for a good one this evening.

(Though I never told you about the rain.)

But let's not spoil it now.

"Sisters, are you still with us?"

Well, wake them up then.

"Could you lead us in a prayer? His sun has set behind His clouds."

Please bow your head.

"All rise."

And I agree, though I must tell you I found Stuart's bottle around the time I began telling you about the dime, remember, and none of you noticed, not even my pencil, and Stuart's excellent fifth is now halved, which makes it a tenth, and Sisters, that was indeed a most beautiful prayer.

Where to now? More questions? Yes, just speak up. And, hey, somebody in here open a window. Hasn't it gotten suddenly stuffy?

"Thaddeus, we've noticed somewhat of a shift here from the story you began about your relationship with Marsha toward—"

Turn on a light. Better.

"—a rather nostalgic stance and preoccupation with your dead—"

As my father always used to say, "From the rear, buddy, step lively now, unless you're a veteran of a foreign war all exits from the rear." By this he meant that if you haven't gone the distance yourself and can't show the scars to prove it, you really shouldn't defecate out your vocal cords. Got it?

The pompous ass. He notices that I've turned down a side-street, and he's worried I haven't a map. I know where I go. Unlike Stuart, who, incidentally, no longer has claim to this fine bottle, seeing how Jo moved out in such a hurry and a huff.

"Too much of Thaddeus around here Marsha take my word oh me oh my you could do so much better and he isn't even a student he has no future he's just an overblown braggart who sweeps the floors in his mother's restaurant and is constantly mooching."

The jealous bitch. Wanting my virtue. Hey, down there. Hanging Johnny, my amazing one-eyed wonder worm. No, wait.

"Sisters, would you kindly turn away?"

All clear, and, my, you're badly wrinkled. What's the matter, son, are you catching cold?

"Hey, somebody. Shut that goddamn window."

Is that any better? Say now, turkey neck, you look blue. Let's bring you over here to the light. Have a closer look.

Say aaaah.

You're in the pink.

Let's have a look at you now.

A bit grimy, wouldn't you say? Hasn't your mother ever told you that you should wash behind your ears? What's that?

You say you've no reason to?

Turn around here, mate, and take a gander at that bed. You know who sleeps there? Sure you do. You've met her a few times, but only shook her hand; you two have never really been properly introduced.

Oh, she's a fine girl. She sleeps there on those pillows. See? What's this? Do you really need to stand up?

Wait. Whoa. Whoa. Nooooo.

Now I'll have to wash your mouth with soap.

How do you feel now? Cleaner?

"Sisters, you might come back to us if you'd care to."

The sinner has been justly punished. I've washed my hands of the entire sticky affair. The toilet paper was blue. Wait—

All lights in the front room work properly, and I'll bet you didn't notice again I had gone. Stuart had to leave us, unfortunately; he was in quite a rush and was looking rather down in the mouth. He splattered once, twice, thrice in the bowl. All we need now is a healthy shit and that would be all the systems working nicely. Mechanic?

"Yes, Mr. Cooper?"

"Air brakes in order?"

"Yes, Mr. Cooper."

"Tank full? Lights? Wipers?"

"They're all working, Mr. Cooper."

"Hand me my transfer punch then."

"I can't, Mr. Cooper. You see, it fell in the soup."

Five nights a week and if it's good enough for them it's good enough for you, eat it, goddamn it to hell, eat it. His brother's idea. Soup will be a growing item, Sarah, your soup is sooo good. After he died, air brakes not in order, wipers and lights not working properly, tank too too full.

Raining that night. Slick. Hot. Summer.

Ring ring ring.

Playing with my transfer punch that night, punching shirt boards, making believe I was driving the old Number 22.

CLARK STREET—HOWARD

"All aboard."

"Thaddeus."

At nine then the pants in the family. But empty cuffs. And him around the house then all the time, his brother, Uncle Karl, Uncle Karl, son of a bitch dirty wet-palmed asshole Uncle Karl.

"Five thousand for you, Sarah, here, as a gift, take it, as a gift."

"Oh, I couldn't, Karl."

Don't touch it.

"As a loan then, Sarah."

"As a loan, thank you, Karl."

Called payment due. . . .

I need a drink. Or something to eat. Cold lima beans in the

fridge. Uggh. Poisoned. Stuart. Still half left. And four cans of that six-pack, discovered in the meat bin. Oh, my reader, please read between my lines.

"Shouldn't keep things in containers, Marsha, especially half eaten."

"But I don't eat all of it, Thaddeus."

"Then someone should eat with you."

"But who, Thaddeus? Now that Jo moved out?"

"Oh, I could stop by every now and then."

"Would you, Thaddeus? That would be nice."

She made spaghetti that night; I remember it well. Noodles thick, clumped. "Looks like rice pudding, Marsha."

"Eat it," she said, "it's good."

"My ma wants you to come over again sometime, Marsha."

"Fine. Hey, Thaddeus?"

"Huh?"

"What do you do?"

"What do you mean what do I do?"

"All day. When I'm at my classes. What do you do?"

"Lots of stuff, Marsha. What do you do?"

"I asked you first, Thaddeus."

"Oh, I do the usual things."

"Like what?"

"Well, I read."

"What?"

"Newspapers, novels, and dictionaries when I can't get crosswords."

"Do you ever think? I mean, about your future?"

"Sure, Marsha. Who doesn't think?"

"Lots of people, Thaddeus. What do you think?"

"About? Just things."

"What things?"

"Just things. And I've decided that it doesn't matter."

"What doesn't matter?"

"Whether I think about things or not. Things just happen."

"Are you serious?"

"Dead serious."

"But don't you want to change things?"

"Some things, sure, if I could."

"You could."

"That's a dream."

"It's a fact."

"Things change in their own time, no sooner and no quicker."

Was that you, Marsha?

I thought I heard someone at the door. Must have a look. No, nothing. Must be the wind. Who opened that window?

It's raining again, my dear reader. Marsha will be soaked. Soaked to the bone. Oh. Damn. Wait.

Marsha, come very close to the page because this is your pencil now that I'm using, your story pencil, the patient pencil having read every old magazine in the waiting room and then breaking its point in frustration and drunkenness, even getting me sick. I cleaned up the mess, don't worry. And I brushed my teeth. Couldn't have a nasty mouth for you when you get here. I used your brush, Marsha. May I bring mine over? I know we need to talk first but we don't have to tell anyone and besides, who says we'd have to live here? Let's find our own apartment, somewhere away from this place, just the two of us. I could sign the lease and maybe I'd even think about getting a job. I can hear you saying that I'm being unrealistic but what is realistic if you don't try new things? I'd get a job. I would. Did I ever tell you my father worked since he was seven? That's a fact, he did. The Great Depression, his father out of work. He had a regular hustle at the train station. He'd go up to the biggest trunk and try to lift it, always smiling, giving them his laugh, a young laugh then, and they'd usually smile and let him take their little bags. Went over very big with the ladies. Lots of tips. Never told anyone. Embarrassed.

Not him or me, but my mother when she told me. After he died. Marsha, did I ever outright tell you that my father died? Oh I make jokes about him, I joke about everything, nothing is sacred, but I'm serious now. He was drinking that night. The night his bus crashed. Or so they claim. That's why there's no insurance. Said it was his fault. And someday you'll die, and I'll die. And then what? So why not have today? Why not, Marsha? Soon enough it'll be all over and then poof, you're gone, good-bye, catch you later, hello maggots. I overlook the frightening part. The knowing it. That's the thing. I wish I didn't know it and didn't think about it so damn much. That's one of the reasons why I like you, really, because you fill your life with so much busy, so that you forget. My way is the opposite. I do nothing and I think about it all the time. I play games. Though a good laugh doesn't hurt, in fact it's good, but games are still games. I wish sometimes I could admit this to you, Marsha. Marsha, you are really a very tender and nice and very decent— That's the word, you're a *decent* person, Marsha. And now after I've broken into your room and sit here waiting for you I agree with everything you and my mother have said about me, that I'm a bum and someday I'm going to wake up and be forced to wake up and oh

I guess I must have been asleep.

Good evening. What time is it? Marsha?

Not here yet. And close to twelve. Oh Lord, what a mess. What a head. A tempest must have struck this room; there are sheets of paper all over. A broken whiskey bottle in the corner. Beer cans. Beans. And, what's this?

Dried up on the rug.

It was the rain that woke me. Beating so hard against the window that I dreamed I couldn't breathe. And the wind— The wind was howling.

My sweet pounding head.

Oh, Marsha—

There was a woman who lay against a tree, and the tree was on a beach, and the beach was near some rocks and vases of flowers, large vases of paper flowers. They covered my father, the flowers, and I asked why he was covered. My father. He shouted hey, son, come out. And I cried here I am, and I climbed out then from beneath the bed, and I looked at their angry shoes and faces, and the bulb hanging down from the ceiling swung back and forth, shining. His badge, 17381, glistened in the coffin. My mother was crying. Thaddeus, come out, she cried. Marsha is out alone in the rain. She lay in the sand with her top off, and when I first touched her she shivered, as if she were very cold. She was afraid, she said. I was afraid when they picked me up and had me kiss him. And his lips. His mustache was frozen white when he walked in through the big front door shouting Merry Christmas, and waiting for me under the bright tree— Was Marsha, and I touched her, and she was liquid. And hot was his coffee steaming in his big red chair pulling down my trousers in front of my mother to spank me, and I screamed. My mother held her face. And when she turned, Karl held her. My father hit me, saying huff, huff, huff.

She said stop, not now, oh not now, not like this, Thaddeus, here on the beach, no, please, not now,

pick him up, there, that's it, he needs to give a kiss, there, he's your father, a good man, give a kiss

to your Uncle Karl, Thaddeus, he is a very good man.

On his badge was a teardrop, my mother's, it shone, I touched it

was wet

like her mouth, warm, dark, hot, secret.

A secret? That's stealing! Oh you take him, you beat him, you teach him, it's goddamn wrong

to do it here, Thaddeus, please?

On his badge was my mother's tear. It shone. And with my finger I touched it. It was wet. The badge was cold. His face was cold. His lips were closed. He did not smile. I wanted him to say *Thaddeus*. His eyes were closed. I wanted him to wink. I wanted him to smile at me. Hear his laugh. Give me a sip of his cup. Steaming. Always were her pots. In the kitchen. Our kitchen. After he left it was others'. My uncle's. Strange people. She smiled. Too friendly. Always tired. It wasn't fair. She was too nice. I became embarrassed. She was not my mother. So I pretended. I am a rough tough mean cool walking slow and thinking fast.

"Good morning, Marsha. My, you look lovely today."

"Shhh. Hello, Thaddeus. You frightened me."

"Surprised to see me?"

"You know I have a test. I thought I asked you to leave me alone today."

"On a nice day like this? I couldn't let you stay here in the library."

"Shhh, Thaddeus. Anyway, today it's supposed to rain."

"What do they know? The sun will shine, take my word."

"Thanks for the weather report. Now, please, may I study?"

"I wrote the story I promised you, Marsha."

"You did? You really did? Great, let me see it."

"You're looking at it."

"What?"

"It's here, Marsha, inside my head."

"That's not funny, Thaddeus."

"You think I should have put it on paper, huh?"

"Please leave me alone so I can study for my test."

"Marsha, hey, you've got time. Let's talk first."

"You say you'll do things, Thaddeus, but then you never do them."

"I'll write the story, Marsha."

"Then go write it. Don't sit here telling me about it."

"O.K., I'll write you a story."

"Fine."

"Hey."

"Hey, what?"

"Why so quiet all of a sudden?"

"We're getting nowhere, Thaddeus."

"Well, do you want to go down to the Loop this weekend?"

"That's just it."

"It was just a joke."

"Everything to you is just a joke."

"Hey, relax. Why so angry?"

"We're finished, Thaddeus."

"No."

"We are, Thaddeus. Face it. We've come to the end of the line."

Oh, Marsha—

Once upon a time there was a boy whose name was Thaddeus, who lived in an apartment in a house with his mother and father, and then with his mother, and finally with his mother and his uncle, who bought a restaurant where they moved into the back room, and who changed things, knocking down more than one wall, and who did not marry the boy's mother, and who did not love the boy nor the father, who tended the restaurant's bar, and who in the back room slurred the father's name, who called him a drunk and said he was weak, and who fucked the mother.

While she tended the steaming kettles, changing from the wife of the father and the mother to the stranger.

So the boy learned change as well, because like the father he was weak, and because he could not kill them, so he began to kill himself.

He was the son of the father.

Whom he hated, because he died and left him, him and the mother, alone and without money and without love, because the father was drunk and weak.

So the boy became a lie.

Until he made the acquaintance of a girl who carried fat

books and who read them and tried to understand them, and with them life, as did the boy, but the girl seemed not to be bothered by the weaknesses in her flesh, and he tried then to defeat her, but he couldn't do it, because she was strong.

And she taught him strength. And he grew.

How he grew:

He wrote a story. It had a boy in it who got drunk and who masturbated and who vomited and who slept and who dreamed and who cried. It had a girl in it who was not afraid of dying. In the beginning the boy pretended to be somebody he really wasn't. Then he woke up and discovered that he was a baby. He stole change from his mother's register and his father's heavy CTA bags. He ate lima beans and walked through a refrigerator.

He found a dime that was really a mirror. He found a pencil that painted his dreams.

He wrote a story:

Once upon a time there was a boy who liked a girl. It was spring. The boy met the girl outside a building at the university. He said hello. The girl said hello. Her arms were full of fat, heavy books.

The girl hadn't been expecting to see the boy. When he said hello she was surprised. They walked about a block together, the boy with a smile on his face, one hand in his pocket, whistling; the girl with a frown on her brow, her arms full of her serious books, out of breath. In his other hand the boy held a paper bag. The girl asked the boy if he could help her carry some of her books. She said they were very heavy.

The boy laughed. The girl stopped walking.

The boy said he couldn't carry the girl's books. But he had a present in the paper bag that might make some of their weight go away. The girl said who is that present for? The boy said it's for a special person I know who really needs it. The girl said really. Her frown grew deeper. She put her books down on the curb.

The boy said yes, then whistled.

The girl said who?

The boy said you.

The girl said oh, and then oh they're candles.

They were special candles, Marsha, and they made the books much lighter, and the girl was very happy.

Then the boy carried his fair share of books.

And Marsha, I wish I had candles like that here to give you. And, of all things, I wish I could give back to my father his laugh.

My father used to laugh, and with his red face and mustache he carried a good laugh, a loud laugh, a really funny laugh inside of him, and he would bring it out sometimes. He would start to smile: at first only the waxed tips of his mustache would quiver, and then his mouth would open and everybody could see it coming, and when you saw the white of his teeth you knew it was in his chest, and it would pick up momentum and speed and grace.

And then his mouth would open fully, and if you were standing just right you could see the back of his throat, see his tonsils quivering and beginning to thunder and shake, and his hands would move quickly to his stomach, and then out it would come in a big, fantastic rush.

And I don't care what it was he was laughing about, his laugh made it funny, even old jokes on the radio or when my mother would tell him that something bad happened or when she would nag him

he would laugh.

And I loved him for that. And sometimes I think that just before he died he realized his death was coming, and I wish that after he did everything he could possibly do to prevent the bus from crashing he had one last fraction of a second in which to smile.

And I wish that his laugh began to build up inside of him, and I wish that it quickly spilled out as his body spilled out through the windshield, and once I read somewhere that sound and light and radio waves and things like that just keep on going and going and going out into space where if somebody was up there with a radio or an ear he could be listening right now to the dinosaurs.

I wish that someday somebody up there would hear my father's laugh at death and then laugh along with it so loudly himself that the two laughs would drown out the rain and the crashing and the thud of his body and the snap of his neck and back.

And may that sound—that person's laugh combined with my father's—go out further flying into all and each and every direction, and may somebody someday hear that

and laugh.

And on and on, Marsha. On and on and on

until that sound bounces off the empty head of God.

And then everything—Marsha, I want everything—I want everything in creation to laugh. Like my father. With him. And that would be Heaven, and that would be Grace, and that would be Good.

Can you imagine that, Marsha?

Oh Marsha, that's why I'm not serious, though I am but I try not to show it, it's too dull, it gets in the way of laughing, it brings me down and there is only so much time and already gone are so many of my years.

It's good that I'm this way, Marsha.

And if you could hear me right now, I'm laughing.

Marsha, tears are running down my face and I'm laughing because I think I hear

yes, it *is* you

I can hear

yes, I know I hear your key

laughing its way inside the door.

The Daughter and the Tradesman

I

She lay in her bed, pretending.

She knew she wouldn't be bothered if they thought she was still asleep. Their sounds were harsh and sudden: one of the aluminum chairs scraped against the kitchen floor; the heavy frying pan slammed the top of the stove. Soon she would smell coffee. Bobbi knew their routine well. She tried to sleep through it each Saturday morning. If the girl listened carefully now she would hear the clanking plates her mother was carrying in from the cold pantry and the tin sound of the cheap radio her stepfather played in the bathroom. Sometimes he sang while he shaved. Or tried to sing. Then he would begin clearing his throat and his nose. Each time he spat into the sink was like a slap. The refrigerator door banged open, then closed. There was the clash of the silverware drawer. Her stepfather spat again. It was disgusting.

She would be foolish to expect better, Bobbi thought, hiding down beneath her sheet, because her stepfather was a disgusting man. Unlike her father, who was dead now. Her stepfather was common: he chewed his food with an open mouth; his fingers were short and thick and always filthy from the dingy little shop where he repaired broken radios and clocks that ran too slowly and rusting toasters that were too tired to pop up. He boasted regularly that he could fix anything. The house was littered with things he claimed he'd fixed, things abandoned by their original owners, things with retaped wires, soldered cracks.

She turned her face to the wall. She wouldn't end up like her mother, a middle-aged woman whose flesh sagged from her body and whose teeth were made of plastic. Was that what false teeth were made from? Bobbi thought. She ran her tongue along her own teeth. Her mother's mistake was that she'd married again; she'd settled for a second-rate, common man. Bobbi shivered. If there was one thing she had learned, she thought, it was that she must never settle for anything less than the absolute best. She believed her father had understood this. He had been born in Europe and was a gentleman. He was a Lithuanian. He came from the aristocracy. He had the best of blood. And that blood ran in her veins too.

Beneath the thin sheet Bobbi stretched her body. It was young and lithe. Her Baltic ancestry had given her fair skin and hair that was light brown, and her features were slight and rounded. She was proud of herself and her body. She was fifteen, and she knew that when she wanted to she could be beautiful.

That would be her escape. Bobbi had a boyfriend, a boy named Tom, a good and reasonable boy from Granville Avenue far up on the North Side, a much better section of the city. Tom was straight and dark and tall. And he didn't go to Lake View, the public school where she went, where the swarthy Uptown greasers and the dumb bucktoothed hillbillies and the Mexicans and all the Puerto Ricans went. Tom went to Holy Cross College Prep, out in the suburbs, and he was in the upper fifth of his senior class and co-captain of the boxing team. He was the nicest boy Bobbi had ever known. It made her feel so important and so proud to wear his ring on a chain around her neck to Lake View; she could ignore all the vile

city boys—she could look down on them—and all the girls
she knew were jealous of her.

She heard water in the sink. Her mother rinsing the dishes,
leaving them for her to wash. Bobbi had her duties. Her stepfather said that as long as she lived under his roof and ate his
bread she would have her duties. Of course her mother agreed
with him. She said work was good for a young girl. Sometimes Bobbi hated them.

She moved onto her stomach and reached beneath the bed.
The dress and the needles and thread were still there. She
would wear the dress today. Soon her mother and her stepfather would leave for the shop, and then Tom would sneak
over, and before that she would carefully shave her legs and
bathe. Bobbi had planned it for so long. She wanted everything to be perfect. She had fixed the dress's hem so that it just
brushed the tops of her thighs, and she hoped that when Tom
saw her he would think her beautiful and sexy. Bobbi had
rehearsed her movements and lines. Acting blasé and nonchalant, she would tell Tom that she wore the dress all the
time, even to school sometimes, sometimes even when she
had to give a class report; then she would show him how she
had looked when she sat up on her teacher's desk in the
dress—she would smile and sit demurely on the dining room
table—and all of this plus the new perfume she would wear
and the expressions she'd put on her face and in her eyes
would make Tom jealous and excited and he would love her.
They would *do it*. And then Tom would never leave her, ever,
because he was such a clean, decent Catholic boy and because
she would have given him what all the boys wanted. No, he
would never leave her. And then he would finish school and
she would finish school and they would be married—maybe
on her birthday—and she would wear a veil and a white dress,
and she would never have to live another day with her mother
and her stepfather. Tom would never regret anything. She

would make a perfect wife. And then for the remainder of her
life, for the first time in her life, she would be happy.
There was a pounding on her door. Quickly Bobbi turned to
face it. She called out, "Yes?"
"We're leaving," her mother called. "It's eight o'clock.
Wake up, or were you planning on sleeping all morning?"
"No," Bobbi called back, slipping out of bed. She hadn't
realized it was so late. "Good-bye," she said. "I'm wide
awake."

II

"Well," Tom said, "who was it?"
Bobbi slowly looked up from a spot near her knee where the
new razor had nicked her skin and a dark clot of blood had
formed. Her hand moved to cover the spot. Her legs were
crossed. She was sitting on the table in the dining room. Tom
was standing in the front room facing her. The late morning
light from the windows behind him framed him.
"I'm sorry," Bobbi said. "Tom, what was what?"
"Whose desk did you sit on?" Tom blinked several times,
and his Adam's apple jumped as he swallowed.
Bobbi put her hand over her mouth and laughed. She
thought quickly. "Oh," she said, "it was Mr. Percy, he teaches
algebra." She didn't know why she chose Mr. Percy; he
was short and drab, and she disliked math. There was something in Tom's voice as well that she did not like. Her fingers
picked at the scab near her knee. Maybe, she thought, she
could tell Tom she did it for a better grade if he asked why.
She waited for him to ask why.
"I thought you didn't like math," he said instead.
"I don't," she answered. She was irritated. Sometimes Tom
could be so stupid; he couldn't even tell when she was lying.

Now the lie was becoming more of a problem than it was worth. But there was still plenty of time in which to mend things, she thought. Her mother and her stepfather wouldn't return for hours.

"Then why did you do it?" Tom asked. He stared at her, then folded his thick arms.

He was still at it. Couldn't he see? Boys *were* stupid. She wanted to get down from the table. She wanted to sit with him on the sofa and be held by him, but she felt unable to move; she felt pinned. She looked at the vase of plastic flowers on the end table. Shaking her head she finally said, "I don't know, Tom. I just did it."

"You just did it?" he said. He sounded like he was spitting.

"Yeah," Bobbi shouted, "I just did it." The tone of her voice frightened her. She felt like she wanted to cry. "Look at me," she said. "Tom, please look at me."

He had turned toward the windows. She slid off the table, smoothing her dress down across her thighs with her hands. Tom turned around and she put out her arms to him, and when he didn't move she said, "Please come here and hold me, Tom. Please hold me. I'm cold."

"Then maybe you should put on some decent clothes." He turned once again toward the front windows, then stretched his arms and back.

"You're a bastard," Bobbi said, and she hoped that it would make him angry because now she was angry and because everything she had so carefully planned was now going astray. She thought about how long it had taken her to shorten the dress, and how she had had to hide it and the thread and needles from her mother, who never left anything private in her room. Her mother sometimes even opened her personal letters and listened on the extension when she talked on the phone. Her mother treated her like she was an infant. It was unbearable. Bobbi was furious.

She glared at Tom's broad back. "Did you hear me?" she

shouted. "I just called you a bastard. Aren't you going to say anything to me, you damn bastard?"

He looked at her and laughed. Bobbi realized then that she had gone about this entirely wrong, and she felt ridiculous. "You did it for a grade, didn't you?" Tom was saying. "You dressed yourself up like a cheap damn tramp so you could get a better grade." He shook his head and made a hissing sound. "You could have come to me, you know. I'm good at math. I could have helped you."

Frustration rose from Bobbi's stomach and burned up through her chest and in back of her throat and her eyes, and before she was aware of what she was doing she had clenched her fists so tightly that her fingernails sliced into her palms, and then she began crying. She felt suddenly blinded and fiercely angry. Then she was aware that Tom had come over to her and was putting his arms around her and drawing her close to him, and she put her arms up around his neck and relaxed, all at once grateful that he was holding her. She felt relieved; she was crying less bitterly; and it was then that she recognized what Tom was doing, that instead of comforting her and forgiving her and understanding her he was trying to unzip the back of her insulting and ridiculous dress.

III

Her father, her real father, had been a tall dark man, thin, with large hands and an easy smile, an indolent laugh. By trade he was a salesman. His name was Constantine Tzeruvctis, and even as he emigrated from the lush expanse of Lithuania he was willing to make a deal: the stony immigration officer stamped Constantine's papers but shortened his last name to Tzeruf; the exchange seemed fair enough. It was a big, new country. Constantine worked his way west to Chicago, sweeping floors, washing dishes, even polishing brass spittoons, and then for the

next thirty years or so of his life he peddled Dr. Cheeseman's
Liquid Wonder, a patent medicine. From door to door to door to
door on Chicago's North Side the immigrant tradesman
worked: knocking, smiling, selling.

All of this Bobbi learned from her mother, from the few
photographs, from the yellowed newspaper clippings that described her real father's death. And like a detective in the pa-
perbacks she had read and the late-night movies she had seen,
Bobbi had attempted to piece everything together. More than
anything, she wanted to know, to understand. But of course
that was impossible. There were pictures missing from the stiff
album. There were questions her mother refused her the answers to. And the musty clippings from the newspaper dumbly
reported only the *what* that had happened.

The girl knew facts about her father. That he drank. That
occasionally he attended baseball games, preferring Charlie
Grimm's Cubs. That he wasn't religious. That both his birth
and his death days fell in September. In the oldest photos her
father smiled and sported a mustache. His discharge papers
from the First World War listed his vocation as Tradesman and
his character as Excellent. His complexion had been Ruddy.
Next to *signature of soldier* was a neat, curly *X,* and beneath it
was printed "His Mark." Bobbi kept the papers in her top
dresser drawer with her jewelry, her letters from Tom, and her
cosmetics.

In her parents' wedding photograph Constantine sat, her
mother stood. As a child Bobbi thought that her father was
sitting because he was dead in Heaven. Later she realized it
was custom. Her mother's hand gripped the back of the chair.
Her father's eyes looked down. Neither smiled.

The first child, a girl, had been stillborn. She was not
named. The gray tombstone in the cemetery read BELOVED
BABY TZERUF. Bobbi saw it once. Green lichen grew inside the
letters. She was born eleven years later, eleven years after her

parents' marriage, and was named for Robert, her mother's grandfather.

By then Constantine was nearly sixty. But when he was younger, oh, he had been quite a fellow. Bobbi's favorite story about him took place one warm summer evening on the Near North Side in an area then known as Bucktown. Bucktown was a tough, tooth-and-nail Polish neighborhood, so named because so many of its residents owned goats. Constantine was young and ambitious, knocking on doors, the dark bottle of Dr. Cheeseman's Liquid Wonder in his hand, when suddenly from the street a shotgun roared. Constantine shielded his head with his suitcase. The pellets were meant for him. He was not hit, but a lantern hanging from the frame house was, and there was a small fire. Constantine began to beat the flames with his jacket. Then the door of the house opened, ever so cautiously, and the barrels of another shotgun looked out at the trades-man's face, and he raised his hands and started to explain. He showed them the contents of his suitcase. He pointed to his now-smoldering jacket. He placed blame for the incident on the Italians or the Negroes. The men then summoned him in-side. While the women tended to his jacket Constantine took out his wares, and before he left Bucktown that hot, humid evening he had made over a week's worth of sales.

Bobbi liked the story because in it her father was such a wonderful liar. Only a Lithuanian gentleman could lie so boldly and get away with it, she thought. She didn't realize the patent medicine her father sold for nearly half his life was so worthless that men would try to kill him out of anger for hav-ing bought it, for their families having used it. Bobbi's mother agreed that it was a fine story. She said it showed how clever Constantine was—he could turn tragedy into success—and how quickly he had learned to do whatever was necessary to get ahead and make a profit in America.

The newspaper clippings described a *dark deranged for-*

eigner on the downtown Washington Street subway platform *waving his arms and suitcase* and *causing a general disturbance.* The police were promptly called. There was *shoving* and *a great deal of noise and confusion.* The man *appeared to have been drinking* and *did not speak in English. It happened quickly,* one witness said. *The foreigner struck a policeman, Sergeant F. Mahoney, on the side of the head with a suitcase full of bottles, and then, when a second officer withdrew his revolver, the foreigner screamed and leaped onto the tracks directly into the path of a southbound Elevated "B" train. The conductor, Calvin Jefferson, testified he could not stop his train in time. The police have launched a complete investigation. The body was later identified.*

This occurred in 1957, in September, when Bobbi was four years old.

IV

There was barely time to hesitate—it was happening too quickly—there was barely time in which to think, but Bobbi realized that she was falling. She broke her fall with her left arm. Then she was on the rug, beneath the dark table, trying to make her escape. Around her was the thick clutter of chair and table legs. Tom was holding her, his arms circling her bare thighs. She tried to kick loose. She was afraid, yet curiously aware that in this time when she should have been terrified she was still thinking coolly, rationally; and as the hands pulled her back she felt strangely proud. She was still in control of the situation. She wasn't crying. She wasn't hysterical. She was still able to function and to think. With these abilities she could handle this boy and his suddenly rude hands, this Tom, her Tom, quiet Tom, Catholic Tom, stupid clean-cut Tom. He would stop if she wanted him to, she thought. He wasn't as bad as the city animals she went to school with. Why, all she would have to do would be to say *stop*.

So this was a game like all the other games, all the at-the-movies games and in-the-front-hallway games and oh-just-let-me-touch-you-for-a-moment tricks and twists. Bobbi thought about the ways she could get boys to notice her at a dance, the ways the boys fumbled in their pockets for a match to light her cigarette, the way they cleared their throats before they tried to speak, the way they pressed against her, trying always trying to get a little further, a little closer, somewhere they had never gotten to before, when all she had to do was to change the way she smiled, to push a hand against a shoulder, to yawn into an eager pimpled face. Oh how they stopped. Cold. Flat. Bobbi knew boys, how they stopped: deflated, tumbled, put down, down, down. Oh, how the boys would tumble. Boys were such silly prissy pampered things, and just as long as she stayed away from the gutter types she could control them, tease them, wind them clear around her little finger, and they loved it. They always came back to her for more because they truly loved it.

How she hated them. Boys were so weak and easy, and finally so boring; how easy it was to predict what they would do. Tom straddled her, kissing her neck. How she truly hated him. She said, "Tom, stop."

He grunted, pawing the front of her dress.

"Tom," she said, "Tom, please stop and get off of me."

Again he grunted.

She pushed against his shoulders with her hands. He slapped her arms away easily. When she pushed against him again he grabbed her wrists and pinned her hands over her head against the rug, and she realized how much stronger he was. She considered whether or not she should fight him. She stared up at the light over the table. A spider web floated between two of the bulbs. If she struggled, she thought, he would have to stop. Wouldn't he? Wouldn't he stop if she struggled?

Then all at once she started to cry, thinking not so much that he was hurting her or that she was so afraid, but simply that it had now come to this, this abject humiliation, this pushing and grunting, and now she would lose both him and something she had always felt was an important part of her.

Behind that, there emerged something deeper, a scary feeling. The girl felt for the first time that she understood something about her father, and she pictured the old tradesman. She imagined him walking wearily from door to door to door, and as she felt the sharp sudden pain of Tom's weight pressing against and into her she pictured her father wildly waving his arms down in the dark bowels of the Washington Street station, and she thought this was how he must have felt when he killed himself. The boy's body above her heaved and jerked. She felt his breath against her face. This was how he felt, why he did it. She relaxed then, holding in her cries. Even though her eyes were shut tightly, the tears continued to run from them. The tears were hot and searing as they streamed down her cheeks into her ears and hair, and then the boy's body finally came to rest, heavily and silently, upon her.

—

V

In the bathtub the girl began to wash herself. At least it was over, she thought. He was gone. He couldn't have left more quickly if he'd tried. Lying on the rug, her eyes still closed, she'd heard him zip his pants and then open and close the front door. He'd said nothing. What do you say? There was nothing he could say. Not even *sorry*. She thought bitterly that he could save his apology for his Catholic confession, and she smiled, imagining him kneeling and beating his chest in some dark church. The bastard. It was ludicrous.

For a moment she pretended she was washing herself with holy water. She prayed the water running into the tub would make a miracle. "Holy water, holy, holy water." Turn me back into a virgin, lift the stain from the dining-room rug, lift the pain, the memory.

Bobbi felt broken. Her insides ached. Then she began to shake her head, thinking that now she was the one who was ludicrous, talking to ordinary bathtub water in a dark bathroom on an afternoon when she should be doing her chores around the house. She had the morning dishes to wash, the kitchen floor to scrub. She could take care of the stain by spilling a cup of coffee or cola on the rug. She would tell her mother and her stepfather that it had been an accident. It would be all right. Sure. She was all right. It wasn't an expensive rug.

She shut off the faucet, sighed, then stood and reached for the light switch above the sink. The fluorescent bulb made a tinkling sound, and then the radio hidden inside the medicine cabinet blared: too loud and too tinny, violins and singing, a man's sudden voice. Her stepfather's latest doing: he must have wired the radio to the light switch. Bobbi shut both off, and as she did she was startled and terrified, realizing she might have electrocuted herself standing in the water in the tub.

The warm water embraced her as she sat. They had never found out exactly what it was that killed her father. If he touched the subway's third rail before being run over by the train, he would have been killed by that. The third rail was electric. Once she had seen a gang of young boys on the Armitage Avenue El platform trying to hit the third rail with their spit, and they had yelled out across the tracks for her to watch them, saying that their spit would sizzle. It made her cry, and after that she always took buses. At the hospital one of the city workers told her mother that if Constantine had brushed the third rail his death would have been immediate, painless. The worker had meant to be comforting. The train had severed one of her father's legs and crushed his head.

Did it matter? she wondered as she washed.

She would have lost her virginity anyway. It was bound to happen, sooner or later. The pain inside her would still hurt if it had been someone trying to be tender, someone she loved. Her father still would have died. Maybe he would have crossed Washington Street and had a heart attack. Or been shot while being robbed. There was crime everywhere, even in the halls of her school. She could have been attacked behind the school or in an alley or in a gangway. She could have been knifed and killed. Her father could have eaten poisonous food or been killed in a brawl in a tavern. He could have contracted some ugly, hideous disease—

No, she thought. She held her body perfectly still. Nothing moved. There was no sound. No, what happened mattered. She'd made a mistake, trying to trade herself. And now there was no one to fix her.

She looked down at her legs. She pretended they were broken. She imagined her entire body was paralyzed, because she'd touched the subway's third rail. And now was the moment when her great efforts would allow her to move. She tried to wriggle her toes in the water. Yes! She was doing it! She was cured! She slowly rotated her right foot, then her left foot. She bent her knees. Moved her head, her hands. A complete recovery.

Bobbi looked at the sink, the toilet, the gray walls. She was aware that she was acting silly, and she tried to laugh out loud at herself—she was kicking her feet now and flexing her arms and splashing sheets of water out of the tub—but instead of laughter a bitter cry came from deep inside her. Bile rose in her throat. The girl's cry echoed terribly in the small, darkened bathroom.

Idling

Sometimes when I'm hauling I drive right past her house. The Central Avenue exit from the Kennedy Expressway, and then north maybe two, three miles. The front is red brick and the awnings are striped, like most of the other houses on Central Avenue. Her name was Suzy and she was the kind of girl who liked cheese and sauerkraut on her hot dogs. She was regular. She went in for plain skirts, browns and navy blues, wraparounds, and those button-down blouses with the tiny pinstripes all the girls wore back then. She must be as old as I am now, and the only girl ever to wear my ring. She was special. Suzy was my only girl.

I met her at a party at a friend's house. A Saturday night, and I was on the team, only I had pulled my back a couple of days before—too serious to risk playing, they said, sorry, we think you're out for the season. I'd been doing isometrics. And though they gave me the chance to dress and sit with the team, I said the hell with it, this season's finished, get somebody else to benchwarm with the sophomores.

Which was O.K., because the night I met Suzy the team was playing out in Oak Park, and had I gone I'd have met my father afterwards for some pizza, like we usually did after a game, but instead I went over to Ronny's. The two of us hung around the back of his garage, talking, splitting a couple of six-packs, with him soaking out a carburetor and me trying to figure if what I had done with the team was right. Ronny told me stuff it, you can't play you can't play. There are things nobody can control, he said. You just got to learn to roll with the punches. He was maybe my best friend back then and I was feeling lousy, here it was not even October and only the second game. Let's get drunk, Ronny said, laughing, so I said stuff it too, there's a party out in Des Plaines tonight. So we got in his car and drove there. Then some of the game crowd got there, all noisy and excited, and I met Suzy.

It went real smooth and I should have known then, like when you're beating your man easy on the first couple of plays you should know if you've got any sense that he's gonna try something on you on the third. I started talking to her, thinking that since I was a little drunk I had an excuse if she shut me down—maybe I even wanted to be shut down, I don't know, I was still feeling lousy—but she talked back and we danced some. Slow dances, on account of my back. And when I told her my name she said you're on the team, I saw you play last week. I said yeah, I was. She seemed impressed by that. But she didn't remember that it was me who intercepted that screen pass in the third quarter, and damn I nearly scored. She smiled, and I held her.

Things went real fine then. We danced a lot, and later Ronny flipped me his keys, and me and Suzy went out for a ride. Mostly we talked, her about that night's game, and me about why I'd decided not to suit up, which, I told her, was really the best thing for me. There's something stupid about dressing and not playing. If they win, sure it's your victory too, but what did you do to deserve it? And if they lose, you feel just as miserable.

I took her home then and told her I wanted to see her again, and all the talking made me sober up, and that started it.

I don't know if you've ever had duck's blood soup. It's a Polish dish, and honest to God it's made with real duck's blood, sweet and thick, and raisins and currants and noodles. Her father, the father of three beautiful little girls, with Suzy the oldest, took all of us out to this restaurant on North McCormick Street and he ordered it for me. He said the name in Polish to the waiter, then looked at me and winked. He even bought me a beer, and I was only seventeen. The girls watched me as I salted it and kept asking me how it tasted. I didn't understand. I said it tasted sweet. Then Suzy's mother laughed out loud at me and told me what was in it. I think she wanted me to be surprised.

Suzy went out with me for her image. There was no other reason, it was as simple as that. Now there's no glory in dating a former defensive end. Suzy went out with me because the year before I had dated Laurie Foster, and Laurie Foster had a reputation at Saint Scholastica, where Suzy went to school. This is where everything gets crazy. Laurie somehow had a reputation, which I don't think she deserved, at least not when I was taking her out. We never did much really of anything, but because I had dated her I got a reputation too, and I never even knew about it. I guess there was some crazy kind of glory in dating and going steady with a guy who had a rep.

She said let me wear your ring, hey, just for tonight, and I said sure, Suzy. And she asked me if I liked her and I said of course, don't you like me? She laughed and said no, I'm just dating you for your looks. I was a little drunk that night and she said do you ever think about it, Mike, do you ever just sit down and think about it, and I said what, and she said going steady. I told her no. Then she asked me if I wanted to date other girls, and when I said no I didn't she said well, I think we should then, and finally I said it's all right with me, Suzy, if you think it's that important, and she said it is, Mike, it really is. She wore my ring on a chain around her neck until she got a size adjuster, then she wore my ring on her hand.

Pretty much of everything we did then was her idea, not that I didn't have some ideas of my own. But Suzy initiated pretty

much of everything for a while back then. Ronny was dating a
girl who lived near Suzy out on Touhy Avenue, and I remember once when we were double-dating Suzy and I were in
the back seat of the car fooling around and she said can't you
unclasp it, and I said oh, sure. And that time we were studying
at the table in her kitchen—her mother was down in the basement ironing and her father was still at work—and she says
not here, Mike, but hey maybe in the front room.

She said hold me honey, hey, and she touched me and I
touched her and she was wet and smelled like strawberries and
her mouth nipped my neck as I held her. She said Mike, do
you like me I mean really do you like me, and I said yes, Suzy,
that's a crazy question I really like you, and she held me and
made me stop and we sat up when we heard her mother coming up from the basement.

The next weekend I bought some Trojans, and Ronny lent
me his car for the night. But before I went to pick her up the
two of us got a little drunk in his garage. Ronny said I'd better
try one first to make sure they weren't defective. He said people in those places prick them with pins all the time just for
laughs, and I said yeah, I sure hope this thing'll hold, and
Ronny said there's seventeen years of it built up inside of you,
remember, and I said damn, maybe she'll explode, and he said
she'd better not on my upholstery, and we laughed and he
threw a punch at me and we drank another beer and then blew
one up and it held good and we let it fly outside in the alley.

The back seat was cold and cramped, and Suzy cried when
it was over, and we wiped up the blood with a rag. It meant
something, I thought, and I started taking going steady a little
more serious after that.

It must have been the next month that her mother started in
on me. She was young then and still very pretty for a woman
who'd had three kids, and she began out of nowhere saying
little things like here, Mike, take a chair, and did you really
hurt your back or is there some other reason why you quit the

team? I had always tried to be polite to her. Then Suzy started to get on me, asking me sometimes exactly what was I doing when I pulled my back, how was I standing, and couldn't I maybe try out for track or baseball or something in the spring? I couldn't figure where they were coming from, and I tried to explain that even before I got hurt I hadn't been that good a football player, that I'd been on the team simply because I'd liked to run and play catch with my father on fall afternoons. Suzy's father seemed to understand, and he'd tell me stories about his old high school team, funny stories about crazy plays and the stuff the players wore that was supposed to be their equipment, and then sometimes he'd get serious and say it wasn't a sport anymore at all now, that it was a real butcher shop, a game for the biggest sides of beef, and if he had a son he'd let the boy play if he wanted to but he'd hope his kid would have the good sense to know when to quit. Because all athletes have to quit sooner or later, he said. Everyone quits everything sooner or later. The trick is knowing how and when. Toward the end I got to know him a little. I'd go over there sometimes even when I didn't feel like seeing Suzy but when I knew there was a game or something else good on TV, and once the three of them came over to my house in the city and the three of us, me and my father and Suzy's father, sat around and shot the breeze and had ourselves a good time, and we must have drunk a whole case of beer, and Suzy and her mother ended up out by themselves talking in the kitchen.

Suzy's father asked me how I quit the team, and told me once he had worked for a guy and after a while he realized he was getting nowhere. He said even though they already had Suzy and needed every penny they could get, one day he sat down with his boss and told him that he simply couldn't work there any longer. He said Mike, there are things sometimes that you just have to do, but you need to learn that it's almost as important to go about doing them in a decent way. I told him that maybe I had been a little hotheaded with the coaches.

He said he respected me for what I did, on account of it showed that things mattered to me, but maybe staying on the team and picking up a few splinters on the sidelines might have been a better way to go about doing it.

I knew even back then that me and Suzy weren't going to last long, and then I started realizing that what we were doing was serious business, especially if Suzy got pregnant. I was cool toward her then. It was around this time that I found out from the guys at school that she had gone out on the sly with another guy. This guy, she told me when I asked her about it, was her second cousin who was having some temporary trouble finding himself a date. I laughed good at that and said damn it, at least if you would've told me I wouldn't have had to hear it from the guys, and we both found out then that I really didn't much care. We had a long talk then, and then for a while things went O.K.

For a while. Until May, until I was walking down the second-floor corridor at school and I got wind from Larry Souza, a guy who was dating one of Suzy's friends, about a surprise six months' happy-going-steady party Suzy was going to throw for me, with all the girls from Scholastica and the guys from Saint George invited too and even some kind of a cake, with MIKE & SUZY in bright red icing written on the top, and me and Ronny were sitting in his garage late one night drinking some beer and talking, and then we were thinking wouldn't it be something if I didn't show, wouldn't that be a real kicker, and then the night of the big party comes along, with me expected to drop by at around nine, just another date, Mike, maybe we'll stay home, sit around and watch a movie on TV or maybe if the folks aren't home we can sneak downstairs after the little ones go to bed and you know what, and at eight me and Ronny are in his garage scraping spark plugs and still talking about it and laughing, and at eight-thirty we need just a drop more of beer so we drive out, and by nine we're stopping by the lake because Ronny thinks he sees an old girlfriend racing down Pratt Street on her bicycle and

I'm saying damn, Ronny, that girl must be thirty-five years old but we drive there anyway and end up sitting on the trunk of his old Chevy sharing another six-pack, still laughing, and then we meet some kids who've got a football and Jesus it's a beautiful night, a gorgeous night in May, and we pick sides and then some girls come along and we ask if they want to play, it's only touch, and below the waist and not in the front, honest, and we've got some beer left in the car if you're thirsty first hey come on, and I'm guarding this goon who couldn't even tie his own shoes by himself let alone run in a straight line and on the very first play Ronny is throwing to him high and hard and the clown falls down and I move up and over him and make the interception, easy, and I'm laughing so hard I stop right where I catch it and let the boob tag me, here, tag me, I'm going nowhere, I'll tag myself, hey everybody, please tag me, laughing so hard and we play until past eleven when a police Park Control car comes crunching up the cinder track and this big cop gets out and says all right kids, the park is closed, and one of the girls says please officer please, have a heart, why don't you take off your gun and stick around and play, and the big cop says sorry, wish to Christ I could, and we all laugh at that, and then Ronny and I say hey who wants to go for a ride and two of the girls say sure, where, and Ronny looks at me and shrugs and I say damn, anywhere is O.K. by me, so we all get in and we drive and drive and drive, nearly all the way up to Wisconsin, the four of us drinking what beer is left and stopping here and there along the road to see if we can buy some more, I'm sorry, come back in three years, they say, and I'm telling this girl who looks like the Statue of Liberty holding up her cigarette the way girls do in the dark car with the tip of it all glowing all about what I did that night, and she says can you picture them all waiting and then you don't show, surprise, and then we have ourselves a contest to see who can guess what kind of cake it was and Ronny says chocolate and his girl guesses pineapple but my girl comes up with angel food and we laugh and say she wins, I give her her prize, a kiss, and damn she kisses back, hard, and then Ronny stops on this quiet road in the middle of the blackness and says hey, where do you want to go now, and I say Canada, and my girl says take a left, and Ronny turns and says what's left, and his girl says we're left and I want to stay right here, and damn that is funny and we drive and drive and drive, and it's long past three and silent like a church when I finally get to my house.

My dad is awake and angry, worried that I'd been in an accident. They called here four times, Mike, he says, and what can I tell them I don't even know where my own son is. When I tell him what happened he says that was a downright shitty thing to do, then he shakes his head and says what would your mother have thought? I think of Suzy's father, how I never thought that he might have been worried, and my father says you should call them right now and apologize. I say it's late, too late to bother them, and he says you're old enough now to think for yourself, do what you do, I'm going to bed.

I didn't call there for a couple of days and by then Suzy had found out what happened. The first thing she said was when can you pick up your ring? I said hey Suzy, I don't want you to give me my ring back, and she said that ring must've cost you forty dollars, and we start to argue.

Her youngest sister answered the door, looking like Suzy must have when she was that young, and you know I bet like her mother too, clean-faced, eyes all shining, with freckles across the bridge of her nose. She tells me to come in. I try to smile to make her smile, but then her father comes down the stairs coughing into a handkerchief and holding my ring in an envelope. I tried to talk to him, to explain, but I didn't know what to say.

Now I drive for Cook County. A GMC truck and mostly light construction materials for building projects. It's not a bad job. A year or so after I finished high school Suzy's mother died, some kind of crazy disease that I guess she knew all about before but didn't tell anyone about, and when I heard I drove out to the house. Her father came to the door and told me Suzy was out. I said I came to see you. He nodded then, looking at me. Then instead of inviting me in he told me that he was busy packing to move to his sister's out East, and then he said he'd tell Suzy I stopped by and that I should be sure to thank my father for the sympathy card he'd sent.

When we'd kiss she'd close her eyes and keep them closed, tight, and I'd look at her sometimes in the back seat of Ronny's old Chevy going up the street with the bands of light moving across her face. And once when we were at the lake she took my hand and said Mike, do you ever just think about it? I asked what, and she said oh nothing, Mike, I guess I just mean about things.

The coaches hollered at me after that interception, like I was a damn rookie sophomore. They said I caught the ball and stood still. But they were wrong—as sure as I know my own name I know I ran. My body moved up and toward the ball, it struck my hands and then my numbers, I squeezed it and went for the goal line. I think about that sometimes when I'm hauling, and sometimes I pull over on Central Avenue and look at the red bricks and striped awnings. I think of Suzy and her father. I grip the truck's wheel, my engine idling.

The Transplant

The forsythia yellowed the northern city's spring, and Luke wanted to get drunk as he lay in bed and once again began to read Melissa's letter. The smoke from his cigarette curled golden in the room. The coffee in the mug next to him grew cool. At the foot of the bed sprawled Peaches, the mongrel retriever, sleeping atop a pair of Janet's dirty blue jeans. Janet was Luke's wife. She'd left in her usual rush of open dresser drawers and dripping faucets—her hair dryer, still plugged in, perched precariously on the lip of the bathroom sink—a half hour before Peaches's sharp barks at the mailman brought Luke out of his dream and to his feet, fumbling for his robe, wincing as he stepped on one of Janet's barrettes hiding open in the bedroom carpet. When he finally stumbled to the apartment's back door to let the dog into the tiny yard he smelled the warm promise of the changing season, and then he saw a jay light at the no-longer-frozen birdbath, and he heard the jay sing its name. Luke thought to put out seed for the jay and for the brown thrashers and the towhees that sometimes came to scratch and the two male cardinals that fought now and then near the clothesline, but then he remembered that this wasn't Virginia, even though he was looking at a jay. This was— Then the forsythia's bright gaze distracted him. He caught his breath. Wagging her tail, Peaches chased the jay away.

In the hesitant sunlight the forsythia stood, a golden shock. It had lived, Luke realized. And now it blossomed. Luke smiled, scratching the hair on his chest. Wait until he told Forrest and Gambino. And Janet, even Janet hadn't been sure. Standing with arms folded, back in Virginia, where they lived two blocks from the Elizabeth River and two miles from the Chesapeake Bay. Paradise. "What are you doing, Luke, will you look at me, are you crazy?" Luke on his knees in the black mud. The U-Haul backed up to the front porch. Her fault they had to move: her life, her career. Opportunity. But Luke said he understood. He went along with it. Dawn, and while Janet packed what was left in the refrigerator and then remembered to prop open the door with a stick he took the shovel and an old sheet from out of the truck and began digging. "Janet, can't you see?" The root ball nearly unearthed. "But it'll die up north, Luke." Writhing worms, the smell of rotting leaves. The dirt dark-green beneath the tips of his fingernails. "No it won't, Janet." Peaches playing trying to steal the sheet. Ignoring the gray squirrel that stole the last of the birds' seed. "I sure hope not, Luke, but I still say you're crazy." Luke bound the root ball in the muddy sheet, then walked for the last time through the now-empty house, smudging all the doors he closed. Below, the U-Haul's impatient exhaust whitened the air around the front porch.

Luke stared from the back porch at the forsythia. The new landlord said he didn't mind just as long as the dog didn't dig holes. She ain't a digger, is she? No, Luke said. He laughed. I'm the digger. Well, I don't want no holes. Chicago wasn't that bad once you got used to the traffic and the crowds and the gray winter sky. The trees with no leaves. The wind and the cold and the snow. Luke watched Peaches run the narrow width of the yard. At first the snow fell as beautifully as the snow on that beer commercial with the Clydesdales on TV. But then it turned to filthy slush and froze. Nothing like a stretch of wet slush to put the old bounce in your step. Joking with Gambino and Forrest at the new agency. Janet was tearing up the ladder, and Luke tried to make new friends. Her working days growing longer as the winter days grew short. Why go home after work to an empty house? The two men introduced him to Rush Street. Warm enough there in the crowded, steamy bars, and after a few drinks—well, you could almost think you were back in Norfolk at a little place along the Bay, the freckled waitress bringing you a plateful of oysters, Janet squeezing your arms as she filled your ear with the news of her new show. How she had most of the funny lines. How she was born to play Noel Coward. How even the assistant director cracked up during the confrontation scene, and wouldn't he come to a rehearsal to give her notes? She needed his raw, untrained reaction. Oysters clean and cold, sweet taste of shell. Janet's high cheeks always flushed when she talked about theater. Her full lips, long hair. Luke's blood thinned as she gradually began to outgrow the town next to the river and the Bay, but when he saw her on the stage— He stared hard at the forsythia. When the curtain rose on Janet she'd be bigger than the theater. Her voice would fill the house. The applause would crack like pistol shots whenever she made her exit, and she never played to them or milked them, and when she was blocked upstage she played upstage. All of it made Luke happy. He had his job at the modest agency, and Janet's popularity helped his sales. After a successful run new clients would call in, asking the receptionist for Janet's husband. And when she was in rehearsal he had the dog and the large yard, his tools and his bags of peat moss in the shed, and throughout the spring and summer there was hardly a day when at least one flower was not in bloom. Luke loved his flowers and each opening night heaped them on Janet. Their life in Virginia had been as full as the ripe figs he let swell and burst on the drooping tree for the hungry mockingbirds who ate the insects that swarmed on the bursting figs.

Disconnected thoughts of morning. Luke inhaled the spring air. His mind saw his drooping fig. It swirled away in the smoke inside any tavern on Rush Street, and as he walked back into the apartment's tiny cluttered kitchen Forrest and Gambino elbowed their way to the bar for another round, and in his reverie he was surrounded by strangers and darkness, and he knew in his heart he was lost.

These hard-speaking, busy Chicagoans. Pale and paunchy in their three-piece suits, always in such a hurry to relax. Making work of having fun, and where did it end, where did it lead to? Blood pressure higher than the Sears Tower. A stroke before you turned fifty. Parking lots and jam-packed elevators, and only boys playing baseball ever looked up at the sky. You looked for a parking space and prayed there wasn't a fire hydrant, and you walked more quickly than the footsteps that followed you down the dark street. And the only green things that grew came in green plastic pots with watering directions, and they paled beneath your apartment's barred windows, and every time you looked up there was another slick, bright billboard, the grinning sexless face of yet another shill.

Peaches paces the length of the fence. Back and forth, back and forth, like the caged leopard at Lincoln Park Zoo. Luke watched her from between the bars on the back porch window. Then he put on water for coffee. How did it begin?

The agent waiting backstage, impeccably dressed. One of those lovely, ageless women, with skin like an Oil of Olay ad. Closing night. *Blithe Spirit.* "Marvelous, Janet, you're just the thing." Janet beamed, then said thank you. The woman did not smile when she took Luke's hand. "You have such a comic sense. Such articulation and timing. I've watched you and decided that you're right for me." "What?" asked Janet, nervously looking at Luke. The woman slipped a card from her leather case. "My name is Mrs. Wescott, I have offices here on the East Coast and in the Midwest, and l know the real thing when I see it." Janet nodded. Luke noticed the dirt beneath his fingernails and coughed. "I place commercial talent." A smile broke across the agent's lineless face. "Lunch tomorrow, Janet, at the Omni?"

The first commercial was a thirty-second spot for Food Towne. Janet wore motley and painted her face. She had to juggle two lemons and a lime, the bells on her fool's cap merrily jingling, while crouching inside a Food Towne shopping cart pushed by an unseen technician down the fruit-and-juice aisle. Her mistakes caromed off the applesauce and jellied cranberries. It took seven takes before she made it past the Bartlett pears and the mandarin oranges, where the cart gently stopped and where she delivered her lines perfectly:

We don't clown around at Food Towne!

Prices slashed to save!

Two weeks later she played a harried housewife who solved her dinner-time dilemma by purchasing a precooked chicken covered with paprika from Food Towne's deli section. The next week she was Eve in the Garden of Fresh Produce, leading a swimsuit-clad Adam by the hand to the winesaps. It was a slow news day, and that one attracted a local reporter and a Mini-Cam. After the station aired the feature, the offers simply rolled in.

Janet hawked Colts and Aspens for Fisher's Friendly Dodge; she draped her neck with pythons and boa constrictors and touted Tidewater's Serpent City. On the radio her voice extolled the virtues of extermination for Captain Ray's Cockroach Aweigh. For three months she was the Grossman's Rubber Radial Tire Girl, popping like a jack-in-the-box from a stack of inner tubes. Then the local contracts stopped. Janet was overexposed. Mrs. Wescott accepted an offer from Baltimore. Luke stood in the corner of their bedroom, watching Janet toss underwear into her bag.

"Don't look at me with that look, Luke. I know what you're thinking."

"I'm not looking at you with any special look."

"Sure you are, Luke. Your eyes are just like Trouble's." Trouble was the cocker spaniel that lived across the street.

"No," Luke said, "I'm just watching you pack."

"I get in the car and there you are with Peaches on the front porch making me feel guilty, and I look across the street and there's Trouble staring at me through the fence with those sad eyes."

"Janet, what did I ever do to make you feel guilty?" He picked up a pair of bright pink underpants that had fallen to the floor.

"It's like Mrs. Wescott says, once you go into this business, business comes first." She took the pants from Luke. "Time is money. I know you want me to start acting again."

"I never said that, Janet."

"You don't have to say it, Luke. Look at how you've been moping around. The gardenias have those little bugs again."

"I know. I dusted yesterday."

"They're beautiful, Luke. You know I love them." Janet smiled. "And I love you. But you can't expect me to stay here and act in Little Theaters all my life. Mrs. Wescott says—"

"Janet, I know what Mrs. Wescott says."

"She says husbands are a liability in this business." Janet stood still. She stared past Luke, then at him. "She says I have all the tools, and great potential. I could make it in the big markets, Luke. I've done nearly everything I can here. But in New York or Chicago—" She rolled her eyes. "I might be able to do a couple national spots. Think of the residuals." She squealed and clapped her hands. "You could quit your job and live off me and do whatever you feel like."

"I'm doing what I feel like now. But things are different. You're an actress. You belong on the stage. You're not a—"

"When are you going to wake up? You know I love the stage, but there's no money in it."

"There doesn't have to be. I work. Remember? We can both live off what I make."

"Sure, and I'll just sit here all day and rot. I don't know about you but I'm not content to stay in Norfolk for the rest of my life." She shook her head, then pulled from an open drawer a pair of panty hose.

"Your acting's very important to me. It was like," he sighed, "like you were up there on the stage for the both of us."

"Well, the commercials and the money are very important to me. I'm good at them, Luke. Really good. And I'm going to get even better. Don't stand in my way."

He didn't. He and Peaches waved good-bye from the front porch. Then he went inside and broke one of his cardinal rules. He called FTD and had a bouquet of gladiolas and carnations delivered to Janet's hotel room in Baltimore. His card read KNOCK 'EM DEAD.

She did. Norfolk, Baltimore, Washington, Philadelphia. Like a runaway locomotive, Janet's career steamed up the Eastern seaboard, whistles screaming, engine barreling past all the stops. Clear track ahead. Nothing stood in her way. Logically her next move should have been to New York City, but Mrs. Wescott decided the train should veer to the west. She'd arranged a top-drawer deal with her office in Chicago. "Pack your bags," the agent told Luke and Janet. "I'm so pleased to tell you that you're going to the Windy City." She left the faint smell of citrus behind her in the room, and while Janet drove to the ABC store Luke called up the landlord to break the lease. Farewell, Paradise. In the yard the pyracantha berries blazed like the tips of safety matches. The rose of Sharon blossoms sadly shook their pink and purple heads. The mockingbirds clung to the fig tree, eating the insects that ate the bursting figs; and Luke pulled off a fig leaf and stared at it, stared at his garden and Peaches, who slept beneath the fence

covered with honeysuckle, until Janet returned with the champagne and two stemmed glasses in her hand.

The morning coffee slowly dripped through its paper filter.
Luke waited in the kitchen, now shaved and showered and
dressed. Saturday. What was he to do? He had those policies
to look over—two hours of work, tops. Janet said she'd be
tied up all day, unless the shooting went quickly. But then it
never did. He took a cigarette from the open pack lying on the
counter and stuck it in his mouth. No, he thought. Not yet. Not
before even coffee. One of the bad habits he'd picked up since
moving to Chicago. He pushed the cigarette back into the
pack. The coffee was nearly ready. He thought about Melissa.

He went into it with his eyes open; he knew that now.
Though when he first met her in the bar on Rush Street he
fooled himself and still thought of himself as a victim. Southern boy forced to move to the ugly, urban North, and like a
Norfolk sailor fresh off ship Luke was looking for it, and
Melissa was willing. She was twenty-three, Janet's age when
they'd married five years ago. Dark eyes, short hair, and blush
on her cheeks that deepened when Luke walked over. He'd
noticed her watching him as he listened to Gambino and Forrest analyze that Sunday's Bears game, and out of boredom
and pure lust he turned to her and nodded and then smiled his
sweetest smile, and when he motioned her over she motioned
him over, and that was the beginning.

At the sink Luke rinsed out a mug. He never meant it to be
more than a one-night thing. Flexing his charm before a pretty
woman in a big-city bar. How far could he get? If Janet could
make it in this city, he could too. He was polite but blatant.
Touching Melissa's hand that rested like a sparrow on the
table, brushing her knees with his beneath the table where no
one could see. Waiting for her to tell him to get lost so he
could return to Forrest and Gambino with the tale of how he

struck out. He expected to strike out. He was surprised when
Melissa agreed to his suggestion that they pick up a bottle and
go to her place, and he was even more surprised when they
arrived there and she put some cool jazz on the stereo and then
sat next to him on the sofa and turned and kissed him.

Of course he'd take a shower with her first. Of course he'd
bring fresh drinks into the bedroom. Melissa could do with
him what she wanted, and she did, and he lay passively beneath her as she moved above him, but then it became too
much for him to bear. He took the initiative. He wasn't sav-
age—that wasn't his style or nature—but he was rather ag-
gressive as he thumped Melissa for all he was worth. Thinking
about Janet, Chicago, Mrs. Wescott. Watching the snow that
fell so purely against the bedroom window, that on the streets
below was changing to slush. When he collapsed upon her he
was relieved the episode was finished and eager to get dressed
and drive home through the furious snow. He wanted to take
another shower before Janet came home for the night, exhausted from her long day of shooting. But Melissa's arms
held him in the way that Janet's used to, and Luke's pretense
withered and shrunk. He slipped from her body. The ice cubes
in one of the glasses on the nightstand shifted suddenly, click-
ing like a thrown lock.

"It wasn't me," she said. "You guys are all alike, it wasn't
me."

"That's not true," Luke lied. "I don't see anyone else here,
do you?"

"Sure, there's a whole crowd of other people here. Can't
you feel them? What's your wife's name?"

"Janet."

"So you *are* married." She shook her head.

He stared into her brown eyes.

"Got a houseful of kids?"

"Just a dog."

"That's sensible."

"I thought you knew. Or that it didn't matter."

Melissa rolled farther away from him and lit a cigarette. "It doesn't, fella. Don't take any of this personal." She tried to laugh. "Most of the time I'm only talking to myself."

"That's no way to be."

She turned. "And who are you to give advice? Christ. If one of us could use a talking to, it's you, big boy. You make a regular thing of this, this cheating on your old lady?"

Luke shook his head.

"First time, huh? Well, join the club. There's millions of you unhappy saps out there, little boys waiting for mommy to turn around so you can sneak into the nookie jar."

"That's clever. Did you just make that up?"

"Aren't you going to be late for mommy?"

Luke didn't know why but he kissed Melissa then. And when the palms of her hands pushed him back, he took her hands and kissed her hands. That moment was the real beginning, he later realized. "I was out with Gambino and Forrest," he told Janet the next morning when he got home.

He poured himself a cup of coffee. December, January, February. By Saint Patrick's Day he and Melissa knew something would have to change. He wasn't getting her anywhere, she told him as they stood on a salt box on State Street watching the mayor lead the parade; and later as they sat in an Adams Street bar drinking green beer he told her he'd take her any place she wanted. Yes, Luke said, taking a deep drag off Melissa's cigarette, I've decided to divorce Janet. Melissa nodded gravely, then said she'd believe it when she saw it. It's more difficult than you think, she told him. Believe me. She patted his forearm. I'm wasting my life on you. She opened her purse and left a couple of dollars on the table, then stood and buttoned her long coat.

"So long," she said. "I hope I don't run into you again."

"Melissa," Luke said, standing behind the table. "Melissa, wait."

She didn't. And that was that, and Luke knew he deserved it. He gazed around the messy kitchen, at the stacks of dirty dishes and encrusted pots and pans piled on the stove. Forrest and Gambino had been very sympathetic. They took Luke back to the Rush Street bar where he and Melissa had first met, and the two men held a funeral, buying a round of whiskeys for the house and toasting Luke's grief and then even having one of the waitresses carry out a shoebox shrouded in black crepe paper which the men then drank to and, many whiskeys later, at midnight, drunkenly buried in the remains of the melting snow. Twenty minutes later Luke stood in the hallway of her apartment building, tapping out "Shave and a Haircut" on her bell. There was no answer. The next afternoon he called her twice, but the telephone rang and rang and rang. Luke grieved.

He grieved, but not for Melissa. He grieved for what had happened to himself. Moping around, even Peaches couldn't cheer him. He mourned a little each day, rationing his sorrow, savoring it, allowing the full impact of what he did to sink in gradually. He came to see that his lost fidelity was less fidelity to Janet than fidelity to himself. If he'd let someone down, he concluded, he'd let himself down. It was a bitter, unflattering thought to accept.

After all, he was Luke, all-around great guy, noble husband of Janet. He sipped his coffee, then opened the back door and whistled Peaches inside. The dog panted happily past him. It meant he wasn't better than the average slob who lied and hustled his way through the streets. It meant he was no better than Janet. That hurt. Even though the forsythia had bloomed this morning, he was depressed. He walked to the front hallway to bring in the mail. The air in the hallway had the in-between smell of coming spring.

His heart banged in his ears as he saw there in the handful of bills and junk mail a letter from Melissa.

There are times when closed doors seem suddenly to open, times when missed opportunities seem to offer you a second chance. Melissa's letter offered such a time to Luke. She was leaving Chicago for a job in the Sun Belt and she would need a roommate. And despite her better judgment she found that she was thinking of him, and she missed his touch. The rest, she wrote, was entirely up to him. He could travel full circle and return with her to the South or he could stay here in the city with Janet. She'd seen Janet on TV, by the way. That Karpet Klean commercial he'd mentioned, the one where Janet did pliés and pirouettes through a jungle of deep nap dressed as an aerosol can. It was his decision; she wouldn't pressure him. Janet was prettier than she'd imagined, by the way. What *was* his problem with her? Was she stupid? Was she no good in bed? He couldn't bring the dog, sorry, because she wanted to live in an apartment complex with tennis courts and a swimming pool, and pets probably wouldn't be allowed there. But maybe there would be room for a small garden. Would he call when he decided? No rush. But if possible by the end of the weekend, because she needed to make plans. She would have phoned him, but writing the letter seemed better, less pressure. She had a bottle of champagne waiting in the refrigerator, just in case he decided to make the move with her. How could he possibly endure living with someone who dressed like an aerosol can? She didn't *have* to have a place with a tennis court and a swimming pool. She was waiting for his call. She'd make sure he had his garden.

Luke sat up in bed and looked at the mess of the room, of his life.

"Peaches," he called. He took a last drag off, then extinguished, his cigarette. "Here, girl. Up on the bed. Here."

The retriever stared at him with her brown eyes and long face, then leaped onto the bedspread. Luke scratched the big dog's chest. "What do you say, Peaches? This morning, should I go over to Melissa's and get drunk?"

The dog listened to the tone of Luke's voice.

"Or should I stay here with you and Janet instead? You want me to pack a bag and leave you, Peaches?"

The dog exhaled sharply, then made two big circles and lay next to him on the bed.

Luke patted the dog's side. He looked around the room. A bra hung limply from the doorknob. Littering the floor on Janet's side of the bed were scores of wadded Kleenexes and a week of newspapers folded open to the comics section. Luke stared at the mess, at three empty boysenberry yogurt cartons, at a pair of rolled-up Danskin tops, the empty arms making broken circles on the carpet. Black banana peels. Wrinkled blouses. Underlined commercial scripts. A THE PLAY'S THE THING sweat shirt. "Up," Luke said, and the man and the dog walked out into the backyard.

Where Peaches again ran the narrow length of the fence, and where Luke stood and gazed at the brilliant forsythia. Like inverted yellow bells, the single flowers. There were hundreds and hundreds of them. It survived the transplant well, Luke thought as he ran his hands down the splayed branches of the flower; and then he turned and searched the ground for crocuses, for daffodils, for the hyacinths and the tulips that were soon to follow. He expected to see their green stalks and leaves standing broken from the earth. But there were none. Of course. He hadn't put in bulbs.

What was his problem with Janet? He thought of Melissa's letter, of second chances. Open and closed doors. He'd closed the doors in Norfolk the morning they moved. Resenting it. Yes. He'd resented like hell having to move, and he resented even more the fact that his feelings were selfish. He had it made; he was perfectly content; he had Paradise. He looked back at the forsythia. It was beautiful in the late morning light. Then they lost it because Janet grabbed for the temptation of Mrs. Wescott. And then he grabbed for Melissa and her bed.

Luke ran to the garage, unlocking the side door. Shovel, the same sheet. Peaches looked at him strangely as he strode back into the yard.

The blade hit the dark earth. The dirt was cold. The work felt good. Peaches nipped the sheet, then grabbed a corner with her mouth and ran with it, playing. He'd dig deep, he thought, wide and deep, to save as much of the root as he could.

Then he sank to his knees. The plant above him swayed in the breeze. He couldn't. No, he could. He didn't want to. The forsythia had survived the winter. Now it deserved to flower and to green where it stood.

Luke stood. He surveyed the pitiful yard. Had he ever looked at it before? he wondered. It was small, but it had possibilities. Peaches lay on the sheet on the brown excuse of a lawn. Well, that would have to be the first step. The grass would have to be fertilized, and now was the right time to do it, when the forsythia bloomed. And this spring he could put in a rhododendron and maybe a bed of floribunda roses there by the corner in the full sun.

Next spring, Luke thought, watching the jay return to the birdbath, by next spring the garden would be brilliant.

The Intersection

We stood in small circles on the grass by the intersection. I
wanted to touch Stacey's hand. It was barely morning. The
sun was just coming up. I wanted to tell Stacey that I hoped
she was all right and not afraid. That I was not afraid. A boy
on the ground was bleeding from his forehead where the policemen had clubbed him. I could still hear the crack of wood
against bone. A girl held a blue kerchief to his wound. The
boy said, "God, Christ, damn."

He was bleeding pretty bad. The center of the kerchief was
stained bright red. I didn't touch Stacey, and then again I
wanted to, and then as I reached for her she folded her arms
and turned. Ted stood at her left. I realized that if I touched her
she would disapprove of me. She would think I was being
patronizing or emotional. This was not the time for emotions, I
thought. Earlier, when the police first arrived, I placed my
hand on her waist as we hurried across the street, and she
pushed my hand away. She looked at me quickly, her dark
eyes glaring, and said, "Lou, don't try to protect me. I can
take care of myself."

I had meant to be tender. But there was no time to discuss it.

The boy rolled his head, still swearing. The girl helped him
to stand. There was a line of blood across his forehead, puls-
ing, open like a bloody ditch, and lots of blood on his swelled-
shut eye and cheek. Some blood had spilled down to his

jacket. It seemed like everyone was talking—there were three or four hundred of us—and we milled in small circles, our backs to the police. They stood two deep in a wide circle around us, bouncing on their toes, slapping their clubs against their hands.

This was the revolution. It was meant to be a turning. A time of change. If the government wasn't going to stop the war, then it was up to us to stop the government. It was that simple. It was a matter of duty, of conscience.

The war had gone on too long. So groups from all over the country would go to the city to shut the city down for a day. It would be a symbol that everyone in the nation would see. Each group was given some strategic spot. The general idea was to clog the area in whatever way possible. Of course the big officials would get to their government offices before the action was scheduled to begin. They'd sleep over or drive in during the black of night. But everyone who worked there wouldn't slip through the strategic spots. Keep enough secretaries and filing clerks away from their desks that day and what in the government could be accomplished? It was very logical.

Still, we knew from the beginning that it wouldn't be easy to seize and then hold the intersection our group had been assigned. We could see it the day before, after we had driven out. There was nothing around that we could use to block the street. No traffic horses or wastebaskets, no scrap from gangways, alleys, or construction sites. Everything that wasn't bolted down had been taken away. The street was six lanes wide, with towering rows of government buildings to the north and west and a grassy area to the east. A small park. There were no benches we could drag. Ted and I checked on that. And we were warned that patrolling the park would be police mounted on horses. The white dome of the Capitol was less than a mile off.

So we'd have nothing but our own bodies. For six wide lanes.

Our tactic would be to keep moving, to hurry back and forth

across the street. Stay in groups. Force the traffic to weave
around us. Slow the cars down. Scurry back and forth. Stop
the traffic.

We had a big meeting the night before. Most of us understood that we'd be arrested, but collectively we couldn't agree
on how. One faction suggested we passively resist. Go limp.
No violence. Make the police drag us from the intersection
like so many sacks of potatoes. That would sure slow things
down.

"Like hell," others said. "That attitude is negative, defeat-
ist. If you move on the streets, you gotta move to win." They
demanded that all of us bring bricks or sections of lead pipe.

The room was hot. I did not like the shouting. So I nodded
to Stacey and then went outside to look at the evening and to
smoke.

We were housed in a church. There was a small library and
ample floor space in the basement. There was not much traffic
on the street. Somebody told us the library belonged to a former speechwriter for the White House, a conservative who had
changed his ideology and now was a radical. They said he
gave up his rich law practice and now defended the poor. They
said the range of political thinking is round, like the face of a
clock. The war made him swing from right to left.

I flicked my cigarette to the curb. The meeting was breaking
up. I really didn't care what had been decided. I watched for
Stacey, and then Ted came out and told me that the women
were still inside, caucusing. I said, "What about?" He
shrugged and said, "Don't ask me, they kicked me out."

He sat down next to me and I gave him a cigarette. We had
driven here in his van. Seven hundred miles. The night was
clear, quiet. We heard the noise from the others who remained
inside.

"Yeah," Ted said, "you know, this town is all right."

"Sure," I said. I laughed. "If you like monuments."

"I mean the scene," Ted said. He looked at me. "A whole

lot of shit is gonna come down tomorrow." He nodded, smiled.

I lit another cigarette. "Yeah." I laughed again.

Ted stood. "Sure would be nice if we could get stoned." His voice trailed off. He slapped his hands together. "But—"

"Yeah." I shook my head.

We both knew that inside there were agents, undercover pigs who were remembering names and descriptions, places and times, who was sleeping with who. Ted knew I was clean. Drugs and politics do not mix. At school there was a big division between the politicos and the culture freaks. We were into direct action and Marxist-Leninist theory, and they were into organic food, meditation, acid rock, vitamin C.

Once I lived on brown rice for a month when I had no money, and I didn't like it. When I ate some meat again I had bad farts for a week.

I continued to wait for Stacey, and when she came out to the front steps she told me she was going back inside to get some sleep. I asked her if she thought she could. She said, "What, go back inside?"

"No," I said, "sleep."

She smiled. "Sure, Lou, just as long as the anarchists keep quiet."

Jokes aside, I suppose I was afraid. What frightened me, simply, was the thought that they might beat me. I was afraid for my groin and my head. I wondered if I was a coward. I wondered if this was how soldiers felt the night before a battle. In my mind I kept picturing the police: their white faces encased inside their plastic helmets, their gloved fists swinging their long sticks. I thought about all kinds of crazy things. Bayonets. Ferocious dogs. Terrible gases that would choke and blind me. I remembered I had meant to wear a jock and cup. I had one from soccer in high school, but when I looked in my drawer at school I couldn't find it.

Inside, two women spoke at the foot of a staircase. One

woman said someday our children will ask us what we did for peace, for human rights, for the silenced and oppressed. The other woman nodded and nodded. She patted the first woman's hand, then opened her arms and quoted Che Guevara. "Let me say, at the risk of seeming ridiculous, that the true revolutionary is guided by great feelings of love."

I slept near a wall on the floor by a bookcase. I slept fully clothed, alone. I do not know if I dreamed. In the morning I drank some cold water and put on a second shirt over my first shirt. I thought that I would be better protected. I buckled my belt as tightly as it would go. Then I loosened my boots and retied the laces.

Everyone moved quickly as we dressed. Someone asked me if I wanted a hit of speed. I said no. I was wide awake. Some of the boys were tying back their hair. One of the women was singing. Outside it was cold and dark. As I walked on the street between Ted and Stacey I was shivering.

A white car pulled suddenly to the curb next to us. The driver rolled down the window, then leaned out. "You fucking punks," the man said, veins bulging in his temple. "Go back where you came from, you goddamn fucking punks."

Ted and I ignored him. Stacey walked closer to the car. "There's a war in Asia," she said. "Does that mean anything to you? At this moment we are killing innocent women and children."

"You don't belong here, get out of this city, you fucking punks." He continued to drive next to us as we walked.

"Blind pig," Stacey shouted.

We turned a corner. The car drove straight.

Ted stopped. He knew the map. "The garage should be on this next block," he said. I looked and couldn't see the group that had left ahead of us. We'd left in staggered groups so we wouldn't attract too much attention. The garage was where we'd decided we would all gather and wait.

"Let's go then," Stacey said. She walked quickly.

The others were inside the empty garage, waiting. Some

huddled in one corner. Others leaned against the pillars and walls.

"You know the password?" someone said.

Ted raised his fist. We laughed. Stacey went over to the women. Ted turned and asked me for a cigarette.

"I didn't bring any." I shook my head. My mouth was very dry. I wouldn't have wanted to smoke a cigarette anyway.

Someone called for quiet. The last group trickled in. "Hey, we need to send out scouts. Who wants to volunteer?"

"How far away is the intersection?" someone said.

"Two blocks. Act nonchalant."

There was laughter. Then others told everyone to quiet down again. "Hey, let's not get our asses busted in a damn garage." For a while everyone whispered.

I walked the length of the garage. I couldn't stand still. Stacey came over to me and asked if I was trying to escape. She was joking. I said I wish I could escape.

"So do I," she said. She smiled, and then the scouts returned, and we joined the others huddling in the corner.

The scouts said they counted seven buses filled with policemen. By the park, east of the intersection. Someone asked if they had seen pigs on horses. They said they hadn't. "Seven fucking buses," someone said.

"Well," a boy said. "Are we ready? Is it time yet to go through with this?"

"Seize the time, off the slime."

"Stop the war."

"Out of the kitchens and into the streets."

"For Uncle Ho."

We moved out of the garage. Some of the others were already there at the intersection. They were crossing carefully, moving back and forth. The traffic wasn't very heavy. The bright headlights shone as the cars drove up the slight hill.

"Let's move," Ted shouted. I shouted something. Everyone laughed.

It was difficult walking in front of speeding cars. You did

not know if they were going to stop or not. We managed to slow the traffic's flow, but we didn't completely stop it. I realized that at various points around the city other groups were on the streets too. We were part of something that was bigger than any of us. History. I felt high. At different times we broke out into different chants, but I can't remember what it was we chanted. The automobiles weaved slowly around the bricks some had brought and dropped. Some of us brought carpet tacks, for the tires, to give them flats. We spread them on the street like children feeding chickens. The tacks scattered to the curbs and stuck to the bottoms of everyone's sneakers and boots. Some drivers shouted at us. Some tapped their horns and raised their fist in support. Some drivers pretended to hit us, but then at the last moment they screeched their brakes and swerved away.

Then the police arrived. The traffic slowed to watch. We grew quiet, cautious. The police approached us from the west on three-wheel motorcycles, sirens blaring. Someone yelled, "Rush them." "Tip them over." "Knock them down." We turned, ready for the charge. They drew closer. We hesitated. All the men on the tiny cycles were black.

We stood still. "Stay in your groups," someone shouted.

The motorcycles began driving around us, forming a loop, herding us like we were sheep. There were only ten or twelve of them, several hundred of us. We could have rushed them easily, knocking them and their little three-wheelers to the ground. We could have used their toy motorcycles to block the intersection, as a barricade between us and the rushing traffic. But because they were black we didn't know what to do. Whoever sent them after us knew what he was doing. We held out our arms, some of us calling out to them, "Brother?" They didn't nod or smile or raise a fist. Instead they drove us into a tighter and tighter circle, like dogs who knew we were sheep who were confused. The dogs herded us across the six wide lanes into the small park.

When we turned and looked at the park we saw the lines of policemen, on foot, coming up out of the darkness toward us, swinging their clubs. All of them were white. The slaps of their clubs against their hands filled the early morning air. Then the buses arrived and more white dogs poured out into the intersection. Then the black dogs disappeared. We realized what had happened. Some of us then tried to run.

A boy was clubbed until he tripped. Then the pigs beat his back and head. Two boys ran across the intersection and were nearly hit by a truck. The pigs chased them and caught one by his long blonde hair. He was thrown down to the sidewalk. A woman's knee was clubbed and buckled backward. The blonde boy's head bounced against the pavement. The crowd turned in on itself. From the center you could only watch. All around was the sound of sticks hitting meat.

We were surrounded. A woman who did nothing was hit full in the face. She clutched her face, then fell to her knees and vomited. Blood ran from her face into her vomit. I was clubbed from behind, in the legs, across the calves. The pain surprised me.

Then we stopped moving. I held my sides and tried to catch my breath. From behind the white dome of the Capitol, the sun started to come up.

It was finished. With the exception of the two buses parked across the street, the six lanes were unblocked. Now the motorists slowing down to stare at what was happening in the park clogged the intersection, and the traffic trickled through more slowly than when we were on the street.

I looked at the boy whose forehead had been clubbed. He was trying to joke with the girl with the blue kerchief. Her mouth made a hard line. I looked for Stacey but could see only her back. I decided not to walk over to her. Then someone shouted for us to go through our pockets and wallets and to tear up everything we didn't want the pigs to get their hands on. Telephone numbers, addresses, the names of friends. Any-

thing that might incriminate anyone. I watched a boy spill out
a pocketful of pills.

"Get in your affinity groups," a woman shouted. "Segre-
gate by sex, and make sure you get in the same jail cell as your
group. Keep track of the others. People, remember they are
your brothers and sisters."

I walked over to Ted. He was my affinity group.

"Lou," he said. He made a V of his fingers and waved them
in front of his mouth. I told him I hadn't brought my cigarettes. He said, "Shit." He kicked the ground with the toe of
his boot. I turned and looked at the rows of policemen.

One policeman chewed a wad of gum and rhythmically
cracked his club into his hand. Another rocked slowly on his
heels. Two others pointed and laughed. They had spread out
their formation. Now they stood an arm's distance apart.

"Well, what do you think?" Ted said. He was smoking a
cigarette.

"Let me have a drag," I said.

Ted laughed. "I guess we're waiting for the buses. Either
that or they're planning on beating us all to death." He
laughed again. "You didn't get hit, did you?"

"No," I said. I handed him back the cigarette.

"There's a woman over there," he pointed, "who got hit
pretty fucking bad." He dropped the cigarette, then ground it
into the dirt.

I nodded. The first bus arrived. The circle of police opened
toward the bus. One by one we were taken and told to stand
facing the bus. Then we were frisked. There were women
guards to frisk the women.

I walked toward the opening. "Was Stacey on that bus?"

"Who's Stacey?" a girl asked.

I described her. The girl shook her head.

"I don't know, man," she said.

I walked back toward Ted. Some of the groups in line for
the buses put their hands on top of their heads. POW's. Ted

stood with his arms folded, still kicking the dirt. "Look," he said. Half the policemen were walking back to their buses.

"Want to try and run for it?" Ted asked. He was serious. The second bus for the prisoners was pulling up now. Some of the groups were lying on the ground, passively resisting.

"I don't know about you," Ted said, "but I didn't come all the way out here for a bus ride. There's got to be twenty, twenty-five more spots where people are demonstrating. The pigs can't bust them all."

I took a deep breath, then nodded.

"We'll run together, then apart." He drew the lines in his palm with his fingers, then made an X at the point where we'd meet.

I nodded again. Ted began to move.

I was right behind him. At first we were walking evenly, blending in with the groups that were lining up for the bus. Then Ted dropped to one knee. He pretended to lace his boot. I squatted next to him.

"You're sure."

"Yes."

"Then let's go," he said, standing. "Now." He broke for the line of policemen. I ran beside him, and then I cut to my right, and Ted was no longer in my field of vision. One pig shouted and another swung his club, but I leaped past them and was running toward the trees and bushes, deep into the park. I didn't think anything was behind. The horse approached me from my left. As soon as I could see it I knew I was caught. I ran to my right. I might have shouted. It came alongside me effortlessly, quickly. My head filled with its smell. In the stirrup I saw the black boot. Light reflected off something. I could hear the animal's terrible breathing and the sound of its hooves on the ground and the pounding of my own breath and heart, and then I felt the club, across my back, and I think I was somehow relieved as I stumbled forward and threw up my hands to block the club as it swung down furiously toward my face. I turned my head. I felt a shock of pain and light, a sudden blinding whiteness, and I know I made a sound then.

I was too numb to feel the other blows, from the two pigs on foot who had chased me. I was relieved because I understood that they could only beat me, and the beating didn't crush what else I felt inside. When they were tired of hitting me, they bound my hands and lifted me from the grass. I tried to look at my second shirt to see if there was any blood on it. I couldn't focus my eyes. Then I was aware that the side of my face felt very wet, and then I realized just how bad I was bleeding.

Ted escaped, though he was arrested later at another action in another part of the city. They put him in the Coliseum because by then the municipal jails had overflowed. In all, that day over ten thousand were jailed. Stacey had gone on the first bus with the other women like I'd thought. She told me later that she learned a great deal from the experience of being imprisoned. She said the women tried to talk and relate to their guards, and inside the cells everyone held hands and sang songs of protest.

My head had to be shaved. They stitched my wounds closed. For a while I had dizzy spells and blinding headaches, and I still have some problems with language and can't hear clearly from one ear.

I don't know what we accomplished or didn't accomplish. I realize now that some things have changed, that some things haven't.

Now we are scattered like the tacks.

World Without End

"Gloria in excelsis Deo," Peter said as he steered his squeaking Chevy down Hampton Boulevard, a Winston bouncing on his lip. Glory be to God on high. It was Sunday morning, Memorial Day weekend, the beginning of the tourist season. Most of Norfolk's residents and visitors were eating breakfast or still in bed, asleep. Lena and August, who had flown in from Chicago on the discount airline the night before, sat next to Peter on the car's blanketed front seat. Lena wore a black hat and was as thin as a bird. Gus was gray and as round as a house cat. *"Et in terra pax hominibus bonae voluntatis."* And on earth peace to men of good will. The old Chevy groaned and rumbled down the street, tires delving into every pothole. From behind a large cloud the sun tried to shine.

"I'm glad my boy still knows his prayers," Lena said, patting Peter's bony knee. He was wearing blue jeans and an open-necked blue shirt.

"You need new shocks," August announced. His hands firmly gripped the dashboard. "We'll never make it to church in one piece. This is worse than a roller-coaster ride."

Peter glanced at his parents, exhaled a thick stream of smoke, shook his head, and smiled. *"Laudamus te. Benedicimus te. Adoramus te."* We praise Thee. We bless Thee. We adore Thee. Pleased with himself, Peter downshifted as the car neared a red light. So far the visit was going well. He

idled in neutral. And he'd do whatever he could to make things
stay that way. *"Confiteor Deo omnipotenti,"* he said, nudging
his mother. I confess to almighty God. Then Peter beat his
chest three times and said, *"Mea culpa, mea culpa, mea max-
ima culpa."* Through my fault, through my fault, through my
most grievous fault. The Chevy lurched forward as the light
turned to green.

"My Petie," Lena laughed. "He's giving us the whole
Mass." She turned from her husband's frown and faced her
son. "So you're a regular parishioner at this church, Petie?"

"Sure, Mamma." Peter flicked his cigarette butt out his
open window and looked away.

"It's a nice church we're going to, not one of those new
ones that look like a gymnasium?"

"Beautiful," Peter said, eyes on the road. "Stained glass
everywhere you can see. More statues than a cemetery, even
more than Chicago's Holy Name. So gorgeous that when you
walk inside it takes your breath away." The Chevy hit another
pothole.

"This ride is taking my breath away," Gus said with
disgust.

Peter and Lena ignored him. "But not so beautiful as our parish back home," Lena said. A furrow of worry creased her brow.

"Of course not, Mamma. Nothing can ever beat what's
back home."

Lena adjusted her hat and beamed.

"A church is a church," Gus said. The blanket beneath his
legs had begun to bunch up, revealing the tips of two springs
that poked through the upholstery. "What do you think, God
cares about the furniture?"

"God cares about furniture," Lena said.

"Yeah, maybe the collection basket." Gus pounded the
dash and laughed.

"He cares," Lena said. "Why else did He make Jesus a
carpenter?"

"Two points, Mamma." Peter licked two fingers and slashed them in the air.

His father's thighs discovered the exposed springs. "Petie, you got to do something about this car. How can you take a girl out and expect her to sit on this? She'll rip her dress."

"Father Luigi still asks about you," Lena said. She shook her head at August, then pointed out his window at a tall magnolia tree. "He says, 'And how is Petie, good old Petie, my favorite altar boy, how's Petie now that he left his good parents and moved down to the South all because he didn't look hard enough for a job in Chicago or maybe because he just wanted to get away from his poor mamma—' "

"Father Luigi says all that?"

"Every Sunday, Petie. He stops us outside church. And sometimes we see him on Thursday nights after he meets with the parish council."

Peter tried a different street. "You're a deacon now, Papa? Mamma said something about Father Luigi asking you to become a deacon?"

Gus wrestled with the springs, his thumbs trying to push them back beneath the upholstery.

"Eucharistic minister," Lena said. "He doesn't think he's worthy." She smiled at her husband, then tried to stop his hands. "He gets up and reads the Gospel sometimes, but he doesn't want to give out Communion. Why should he, he's no priest."

"Things change, Mamma. That's legal now."

"It used to be a mortal sin and now they even let Nick Guiliani touch the Host." Nick Guiliani owned the neighborhood Shell station. "Whenever I see him passing it out with his greasy hands I change lines. Don't we, August? Holy Communion should come from a priest, not Nick Guiliani."

"Before you open your mouth, Mamma, you could whisper, 'Hey Nick, fill her up!' "

Gus chuckled as Lena said, "You take it in your hand, Petie. I'll do it the old way with Father Luigi, but when I get stuck in a line with an ordinary person I take it in my hand. You don't know if they wash."

"It still goes in your mouth, Mamma."

"Yeah, but I give the germs time to jump off on my hand." Lena nodded and looked at her hand. "We talked all about it one night during parish council. Your papa thinks I'm crazy."

"What did Father Luigi say?"

"He thought she was crazy too," Gus said.

"No he didn't," Lena said. "He changed the subject. Whenever I talk to him, he changes the subject. That was the night he first asked me about you."

Peter turned back toward Hampton Boulevard. Azaleas of all colors bloomed in front of the houses lining the streets. Absently Peter said, "So what did you tell him about me? Good things?"

Lena stared at her hands, her lap, the car's roof, out the windshield, all the time shrugging and looking hurt and sad. Peter realized his mistake. He gave the Chevy gas.

"What could I say, Petie? What can a mother say? That her son doesn't think the upstairs flat is good enough for him, His Royal Highness, so he has to move out into a dangerous neighborhood full of hoodlums and ends up wasting half of his paycheck on rent?"

"Mamma, that was nearly two years ago."

"Let me finish. You asked me a question, so the least you could do is hold your breath until I'm finished." Peter reached across the dash for a cigarette. August's thumbs again fought the springs. Lena nodded her head and smoothed her dress. "That's only the tip of the iceberg, my son. Don't think anything you do ever escapes your mother's eyes."

"Lena," Gus said, "get to the point."

"Don't be in such a hurry, Augusto." Lena called her husband Augusto only during arguments. "You're on vacation now. You unloaded trucks fifty weeks for this. Relax. Re-

member, the doctor told you you don't have a strong heart."
The Chevy bounced over another pothole. "Your son throws
away his good money on an opium den on South Halsted and
you don't think his mother sees? Then he met that girl— That
stewardess— That hussy—"

"Lorraine wasn't a hussy, Mamma."

"She moved in with you, didn't she? You didn't marry her,
did you? What do you think, I was born yesterday? I don't
want to open old wounds, but you had only one bed in that
apartment, Petie."

"You'd actually take a girl out in a car like this?" Gus had
succeeded in getting the springs beneath the upholstery, but
the last bump popped them out again. "I can't believe it. I
wouldn't be caught dead. She'd have to wear a suit of armor."

"*Dominus vobiscum,*" Peter said. The Lord be with you.
"*Et cum spiritu tuo.*" And with thy spirit. With his right hand
Peter made a broad sign of the Cross over the steering wheel.

"But then she got wise," Lena said, "and never came back
from a flight to Albuquerque."

"Tucson," Peter said.

"What's the difference?" Lena said. "You gave her some
thrills, and the hussy packed her bags. So you had your fun,
some pleasure, a little enjoyment."

"Lena," Gus said, "it's a Sunday. Don't describe."

"It's only natural, Augusto. We raised a healthy boy. His
blood is red like everyone else's. Just as long as he doesn't get
disease. Don't pretend to be such an innocent."

"The church is around here somewhere," Peter said, taking
a drag off his cigarette and letting out the clutch.

Gus pointed to his heart. "Me? Pretend to be an innocent?
Lena, I'm more faithful than Lassie. You believe too many of
Monty's stories."

"I know you served your country, Augusto, but you were
stationed in France for two years. I go to movies. I'm a mod-
ern woman. I wasn't born with blinders on my eyes."

"Maybe it's the next block." Peter exhaled a line of smoke.

"I've never strayed," Gus said. "Even before I met you I was faithful. I swear to God. Nowadays I don't even look."

"Oh, I could see what Little Miss Airlines was doing to our Petie." Lena turned to her son. "First you grew that ugly mustache. Then you started wearing those stupid clothes. How can you sit down when your pants are that tight? And you wouldn't button all the buttons on your shirts. Was it the thin air up in the clouds that made her think that was sexy? Then you lost so much weight I thought we'd have to put you in the hospital. Didn't she know how to cook? I know you had a stove, I cleaned it with my own hands. But I suppose the kitchen was too far away from the bedroom."

"Lorraine was a vegetarian, Mamma."

"I cook vegetables. August, tell Petie that I cook vegetables."

"Petie, she cooks vegetables."

"What you need is to come back to Chicago where you can meet a good clean Catholic girl. Somebody like Rosamaria D'Agostino."

"Mamma, Rosamaria D'Agostino joined the Carmelites. She teaches kindergarten in South Bend."

"Are you sure you know where this church is?" Gus said.

"She would have married you if you asked her," Lena said. "God was her second choice."

"There's a church," Gus said, pointing beyond the windshield.

"That's a post office," Peter said, "and Rosamaria D'Agostino wouldn't have married the Pope. Even back in second grade she wanted to grow up and become a saint. The rest of the kids talked about being cops or firemen or astronauts, but not Rosamaria D'Agostino. She even had picked out her own feast day." He made a turn at 38th Street and tossed his cigarette out his window.

"Some children are blessed with ambition, Petie," Lena said. "Others need a little time to grow, settle down, mature. You could take a page out of her book, you know."

"But you always told me someday you wanted grandchildren."

"You could make plans, Petie."

"I know. Wake up, smell the coffee."

"The early bird eats the worms."

"Remember the Alamo. Tippecanoe and Tyler too." Peter turned, heading back toward Colley Avenue. *"Benedicamus Domino."* Let us bless the Lord.

"You had such promise, Petie." Lena snapped open her purse. She shook her head sadly. "Three merit badges short of being an Eagle Scout. Second soprano in the fifth-grade choir. Sergeant of the Saint Felicitas patrol boys. Captain altar boy. Then in high school you were president of the Camera Club. We were so proud. And all of your science projects, Petie. Remember how you used to cut up those ugly worms? We still keep your jars and ribbons in your old room." Lena held a round mirror before her face as she spread on a fresh layer of lipstick. "Remember how proud we were when they printed the news in the parish bulletin? We thought maybe you'd get a college scholarship. We thought you'd find the cure to cancer. Work with test tubes and one of those fancy electronic microscopes, go to your job every day wearing a white coat and a tie. Ah, a mother's hopes and dreams. I knew they were all down the drain the day you flunked out of junior college."

"I dropped out, Mamma."

"We're family, Petie. You flunked out. Don't be polite."

"I wear a tie to work, Mamma."

"You wear a tie. The crazy Albanian who runs the fruit stand up on Clark Street wears a tie." Lena put her mirror and lipstick back inside her purse. "Whenever the ladies come in he smiles and pinches the cucumbers." She blotted her lips with a tissue. "That's all men think of nowadays. I tell you, son, that girl ruined your life. Just look at you. Why can't you at least shave off your mustache?"

Peter braked suddenly at a red light on Colley. "Papa, did you ever feel like giving someone we know and love a little punch?"

"Petie!" Lena said, one hand flying to her breastbone, the other brushing the top of her black hat.

Gus stared out the window, then turned to Peter and smiled. "That's a good question. Don't think I was never tempted. But what good would it do? I'm not a brute. I once knew a man who hit his wife—remember Sal, Lena? The time he raised a hand to Sophie? We visited him in the intensive care. He couldn't carry on a conversation because of all the tubes in his mouth and nose, so we'd stand by his bed and say, 'Hello, Sal, we hope your bones set, we hope the doctors can stop the bleeding. The priest is on his way to give you the Last Rites.' " Gus laughed. "They were boring visits. All Sal could do was gurgle." He caught Peter's eye, then nodded at Lena. "A man lives and learns. Are you taking us to church, Petie?"

"Of course, Papa." Peter revved his engine. "Why?"

"Because unless I'm seeing things we already drove past this post office." He pointed again beyond the windshield.

The Chevy roared across the intersection. Lena stared straight ahead, her arms folded atop her purse. She seemed made of stone or ice. The engine popped and whined as Peter put it through its gears. "There are an awful lot of post offices down here in the South, Papa. And every one looks alike. I figured I'd take the scenic route and show you some of the sights. We'll get to the church in no time."

"Messenger boy," Lena said finally.

"What?" Peter and Gus said, surprised.

"Messenger boy. Flunky. Lackey. That's what I raised. A stooge. Big deal, so he wears a tie, maybe even a nice pair of dress pants, not that he puts them on when I come a thousand miles to see him. So he has clean hands. But he's still somebody's errand boy."

"I'm a courier, Mamma."

"You're one of the Three Stooges. The stupid fat one they hit all the time in the face. Oh, I never liked that show. And I never liked those Marx Brothers, honking their horns at innocent women and walking all over good furniture and throwing pies in your face." Lena took a deep breath. "So your papa should hit me? I'll show you hit, Petie boy. Pull over. Augusto, hand me your belt. He's not too old to beat."

"The boy didn't mean anything—" Gus began.

"Augusto, he showed disrespect." Lena swallowed. "Take us to the airport. We're going home."

Peter drove, his mother's words falling around him like slaps. In the sky a pair of seagulls squealed and soared. "Mamma," he said, "Mamma, I've always tried to do my best. It wasn't my fault I couldn't find a job in Chicago. I looked. I tried. But when Lorraine didn't come back from Tucson I felt devastated." He glanced at Lena to see if she was softening. "Mamma, I was hurt. I was abandoned. I was lonely and without love."

Gus rolled his eyes. "There's a church. Or is it another post office?"

The Chevy bounced forward, free of stop signs, red lights. "I thought about becoming an alcoholic, Mamma, and then I considered trying marijuana, paint thinner, Coke and aspirin. At night I walked the rainy streets, hoping I'd get mugged. I was broken and shattered, Mamma. I even thought about committing the unforgivable sin of suicide. I figured I'd cross State and Madison in front of a taxicab, or I'd blow out the pilot and put the oven on broil."

"There's one," Gus said. "No, it's Southern Baptist."

"I thought about swallowing razor blades, Mamma. Jumping off the Hancock. Going to a White Sox game and telling everyone I liked the Yankees. But then one night I heard a church bell ring, and I thought about your love."

"Go on," Lena waved. She unsnapped her purse, found a tissue.

"Yeah," Peter said, "it was nearly noon and the church bells—"

"You said it was at night."

"Episcopalian," Gus said, "or else a fire station."

"I mean it was midnight, Mamma, and I felt so low I could have gone into a grocery store and eaten a jar of Ragu."

"Ugh!" Lena said. "Cat food! Change the subject before I'm sick."

"Your love saved me, Mamma."

"So that's why you moved away, Petie? You don't make sense."

"No, Mamma, no, I moved to get experience. They told me at all the job interviews I didn't have enough experience. Someday I'll move back."

"Catholic, Petie! Roman Catholic! Look, a crucifix and everything! Stop the car!"

"Petie, why didn't you ever tell me?" Lena dabbed her eyes.

Peter pulled over to the curb, tirewalls scraping the concrete. "You never asked me, Mamma. You assumed it was because of Lorraine."

Gus had opened his door and was untangling his legs from the blanket, his trousers from the springs. Lena patted her son's head. Even though the engine was shut off, the Chevy knocked and sputtered and coughed.

"She was a nice girl, Petie, maybe a little too thin and too stuck up with her nose in the clouds, but she was a pleasant girl to talk to. Still, she wasn't the right girl for you."

"I know, Mamma. But a man's got to have experience." He helped his mother slide out of the car.

"You'll have to tell us more about your job. You deliver important things, like telegrams and legal contracts?"

"Not telegrams, Mamma. Actually I deliver interoffice communications. But my job requires responsibility and punctuality."

Lena smiled. "Those are nice things, Petie."

"Mass starts in five minutes," Gus said, returning to the car. "Is my hair combed?" He touched his wife's elbow. "Do I look all right?"

Lena licked two of her fingers and smoothed her husband's hair. "It's a nice church, Petie, not one of those new ugly ones?"

Gus walked behind his son, checking his hair in the side mirror.

"It's beautiful, Mamma." Peter had never seen the church before. "I come here every Sunday."

Lena laughed. "Of course you do. Starting today." She pinched his cheek. "Right after Mass we'll introduce ourselves to the pastor and sign you up." She smiled and turned. "August, don't waste so much time. We don't want to walk in late."

Gus wagged his head.

"Walk on this side of me, August."

"Coming, Lena."

"Introibo ad altare Dei," Peter said. I will go unto the altar of God. *"Ad Deum qui laetificat juventutem meam."* To God who giveth me joy to my youth.

"And you walk on this side, Peter." Lena was smiling. The bright morning sunshine spilled their long shadows across the sidewalk. "I want us to enter the church together, like one big happy family."

The shadows swam together as Peter took his mother's arm, then kissed her cheek. *"Sicut erat in principio, et nunc, et semper: et in saecula saeculorum."* As it was in the beginning, is now, and ever shall be. World without end.

The Walk-On

In the beginning Nick sits in a second-row desk, the first day of a fall semester sophomore speech class, eagerly tapping his feet and chewing bubble gum. He stands when the instructor nods to him, jogs to the front of the room, cocks his baseball cap, then leans over to get the catcher's signals. He shakes off the first sign. Then he straightens, going into his windup, and says, "My name is Nick DiSalvo. I'm last year's walk-on from Chicago, the kid who earned the scholarship, the fourth starter. I'm pleased to meet you all." The class smiles. The instructor nods. Nick looks around and then sits back down.

Anne watches from the fifth row, sitting near the on-deck circle in the sun. Nick turns as the instructor points to her, hears the swish of her nylons as she stands, hears the roar of the crowd, hears her step lightly across the room to the plate and softly clear her throat.

"I'm Anne Chambers," she says. "I'm your average beautiful girl, but Nick, if you sit next to me, I'll become something very special, and in the end I'll break your heart."

The class smiles. Nick smiles. Anne smiles. Nick moves his desk next to hers the following day.

The ending takes place during the spring of Nick's senior year, just outside the Student Union, while Nick is heading through the midday change of classes toward the Administration Building to try to take out another student loan. Nick sees Anne walking down the Union's back steps. He starts to walk away, then stops. He waits for her to come over and say hello to him. Anne's arms are full of books—her skin seems to glow but she looks heavy—and her eyes are lined and worried.

They smile nervously and talk. She about her studies, papers, tests, and he about his season, how tough it is this year without a scholarship, how he has lost his fastball, how he is no longer the fourth starter. He offers her some bubble gum but she refuses. When he leaves he says, "Take care, Anne, I'll see you around."

Anne says, "No, Nick, probably not," and waves.

She is correct.

For both die that day. Nick, on his way to the third-floor Office of Student Loans, just outside the second-floor Office of Athletic Scholarships, of a severe fall down the cold marble steps of the Administration Building, after slipping on a banana peel, of a concussion, a contusion on the brain. And Anne by a falling meteor, on the corner of Sixth Street and Race, a short cruel block away from her apartment, her lined and worried eyes indented by the visitor from outer space, a case for the insurance companies and the record book.

In Fort Gordon, Georgia, Lt. David Michael Harper is cleaning his rifle behind his barracks when a private shouts out and David turns his head, then stands and takes a step around the corner, onto a seldom-used driveway, but into the path of a supply truck speeding its way from the enlisted men's cafeteria. The right front fender bumps Harper's body. Harper's head bounces on the pavement. This accident goes to court.

It is a day for death. Which does not actually happen.

But Nick DiSalvo wishes it had, wishes he were the manager of his own team, wishes he could make out the lineup, write the substitutions in at will. It is December, a cold and very lonely seven months after the day outside the Student Union, and Nick is in Chicago walking up the steps to his third-floor apartment. Nick pretends he is ascending the pitcher's mound, pretending the mound is made of marble. He sees the banana peel out of the corner of his eye, he thinks of Anne—it is too late—she turns and waves, he slips and falls. At the second flight of steps Nick imagines the meteor as it burns a hot white trail across the blue Illinois sky, then rushes down through telephone wires, through the tops of trees, through twigs and budding leaves, through Anne's upturned head. In his apartment he sits at the edge of his bed and reaches for a cigarette. His foot presses down the imaginary accelerator. He pushes in the lighter on the dashboard and neatly shifts into third. Nick hears the click of the lighter as it pops out, he sees the shining grill, the crushed bodies of a thousand and one Georgia insects on the supply truck's radiator, then Harper falls, backward, clumsily, onto Nick's bed, dead.

Nick lives the middle of the story. He lives it each day as he wakes, as he throws himself to the floor to do his morning push-ups, as he brushes his teeth and then spits foam into the sink, as he goes outside to run and to buy the morning paper. Nick works nights now. He is a bartender at a place called The Second Fiddle, on Broadway Avenue in New Town, the newest of four regulars. He is given all morning and afternoon to think of meteors, to plot trajectories, to situate banana peels, to accelerate heavy trucks. Always it is a meteor, though sometimes it gives out the private's shout, swinging south over Georgia before it settles on Sixth and Race in Champaign. Sometimes the banana is a carrot—the truck, a motorcycle. This morning in gray and cold December Nick is adding another variation. The meteor, the banana peel, and the speeding supply truck are each carrying notes.

"Hey," the notes read, "we need some help out here!"

Nick wonders if Anne would have time to read it. If the meteor yells to her as well, perhaps she'd have time to look up. Time to make out the dark letters between the leaves. Time to get the general idea. Time to realize, at least, who the message is from.

It is from Nick DiSalvo, on the mound for the University of Illinois Fighting Illini, the skinny, cocky walk-on who not only makes the team his first year out by striking out seven Purdue Boilermakers in a row during a freshman game but is given a varsity scholarship and the fourth-starter job his second year, looking adequate against Ohio State, respectable against Iowa, fantastic against Minnesota, only to lead the Big Ten in total walks and hit batsmen his third season, and to lose his scholarship and his starting role during his fourth. Sitting out in the bullpen, Nick the freshman smiles and autographs scorecards, gets the nod during the fifth inning of the second game and jogs to the mound, mows down fourteen consecutive Indiana Hoosiers, bringing the lazy shirt-sleeve crowd to its feet. Nick the sophomore breaks out unevenly from the pack, he struggles, loses his first start against the Badgers of Wisconsin, but then he finds his groove, pitches a clean three-hitter against Michigan. As a junior Nick worries, he snaps his bubble gum and frets, he hits everybody—opposing pitchers, four Northwestern Wildcats in succession in the bottom of the ninth of a close game, even the umpire once, once even Anne's roommate Bev, his fastball tailing up and around and into the stands. Nick the senior starts his last season riding the bench, he picks up his share of splinters, he jokes to the sophomores about always having the toothpick but never the bite, the desire, the catsup and mustard and relish to win the big one.

Against the Spartans of Michigan State in his final appearance, Nick is surprised when he escapes the first inning undamaged, is relaxed until the third when he gives up a hit and a walk, and then he balks.

His catcher plods to the mound. "You got problems today, DiSalvo?"

"Tell me about it," Nick says. He squeezes the baseball and wipes his forehead, his eyes searching the stands for Anne.

"Keep 'em low," says the catcher.

And Nick nods, decides to get tough, decides to pitch his heart out. He fans the next two batters, then gets the third on an easy grounder. He surrenders a double in the fourth but doesn't let the man across. He strikes out the side in the fifth, fans two out of three in the sixth, his fastball back, his eyes still searching, the game still scoreless. Until the rain.

"Guess who wins this one?" The catcher shrugs, spits. Dark puddles blotch the field.

Nick doesn't want to leave the dugout. "It isn't fair," he says.

"No shit. We should have scored some for you."

"But we didn't."

"We sure had our chances. No shit."

"It just isn't fair."

"You pitched real well. You had this game, DiSalvo."

"A meaningless rain-out."

It is evening.

Nick relives the middle of the story. He dresses and heads for The Second Fiddle, he walks briskly out into the clear December air, he leaves Speech 201 class with Anne on his arm.

"Nick," Anne says, "I have to mail a letter."

Nick sees the blue and red stripes on the sides of the envelope. Anne looks straight ahead. Nick thinks, wonders, speculates, stops on the bicycle path just outside busy Lincoln Hall, near the library and the street. He squats and takes a deep breath.

Anne stops too, in the middle of the street. The traffic slows, honks, weaves around her. A three-speed brushes Nick's pitching arm.

"What's the matter, Nick?" Anne says.

Students begin to gather. Several motorists on Wright Street turn off their engines to watch. Librarians pour out of the library, squinting in the bright sunlight. The passing Illini cross-country team slows to a standing-in-place trot.

"Nick?"

He folds his hands, then opens them. His eyes move back and forth. He moves his lips, he appears to read, there is no sound. He sways.

"Hey, Nick?"

A pigeon lights on his shoulder. In the distance there are sirens.

"Miss?" a librarian calls out. "Yes, you there standing in the middle of the street. I think that boy wants you to read him your letter."

Nick nods. Anne groans and shakes her head. The crowd of students, trotting cross-country men, motorists, bicycles, and wheelchairs begins to chant. "Read that boy the letter."

Anne pinches her eyes, then rips open the envelope. There are cheers.

" 'Darling David,' " Anne reads, then stops.

"Loudly now," the librarians call out.

" 'Darling David, I want you to know that while you're down in Georgia fighting for the freedom of this country I miss you and I love you. And I've been thinking about the night when you proposed. I'm still too young, I think, to consider marriage. But your words are always on my mind. You should be happy to know that I'm casually dating, just like we agreed both of us should during this difficult time of separation. I met this guy in my speech class—his name is Nick. He's a baseball player, the walk-on who got the big scholarship. He could be really good. I haven't told him about you yet. That's all for now. Love, Anne.' "

Nick stands, rinsing another beer mug. The manager yells over to him to hurry up. As usual The Second Fiddle is crowded—packed like the grandstands on Ladies Day, Nick thinks. He nods, waves his dripping arms, then mumbles to himself and anyone within earshot the morning's message, "Hey, we need some help out here."

"Sure, but you'll have to pour me a drink first."

A customer. Blonde, attractive, probably twenty-two or twenty-three. Nick asks anyway to see some I.D. Her name is Vicky Williams.

"Good evening," Nick says.

"Good evening to you too, and if you're through dreaming I'll have a Canadian Club on the rocks."

Nick reaches for the whiskey. "Peanuts?" he asks. Vicky takes a dollar from her wallet and says yes.

"Shell 'em yourself, miss." He sets the basket of nuts on the bar.

"You're a strange one," Vicky says.

"I'm just a ballplayer without a following, miss. She jilted me for a first lieutenant."

"I was jilted for the girl who lived next door."

"To you or to him?"

"Actually both. I lived two doors down."

Nick turns and rinses more beer mugs. He refills peanut baskets. He empties ashtrays, he tells a joker not to sit on the jukebox, he tosses away dead beer bottles and opens cold fresh ones, he wipes up ashes, suds, shells, occasional nickels and dimes from the bar.

"Hey, ballplayer," Vicky says, later, tugging Nick's arm. "Remember me? What time do you knock off?"

"I work until the final inning, or at least each night I try to."

"Can I catch you later in the parking lot?"

Nick nods.

Anne holds her head and cries. They are in Nick's basement apartment on Main Street, two months after they have met, smoking cigarettes, listening to the radio, sitting naked on Nick's rumpled bed.

"It was that bad, huh Anne?" Nick asks.

She sobs. He stands and turns off the radio. Then he walks into his kitchen, finds and puts on his cap, winces and stares at the refrigerator. Nick shakes off the first two signs. Then he winds up, delivers, hears the grunt of the batter, the crack of the bat. The manager runs out and hands Nick the towel. Nick stares at his glove and heads for the showers, thinking he'll need a computer to figure his mushrooming ERA.

"I've been laughed at," he calls to Anne, "I've been slapped in the face, I've been booed. Once a girl even fell asleep in the middle of it—" He walks back to the bedroom. "But never this, Anne. Never tears."

"You don't understand, Nicky."

"Nick. The name is Nick. The diminutive of Nicholas. From the Greek, meaning 'victory of the people.' "

"This afternoon you earned your victory, Nicholas." Her eyes widen.

Nick pauses, confused. "The full nine innings, Anne? Victory? No need for a reliever?"

"No need for a reliever, Nick. You just pitched a shutout, a perfect game, a no-hitter."

"Then why the tears?" He scratches his cap. "You rounded third and headed for the plate but didn't score, eh Anne?"

"I scored. Believe me, I scored. Remember when my legs tightened?"

"I thought you were just trying to stay awake."

"I still tingle, Nick."

"Stop. You'll make me blush."

"Go ahead and blush. This was my very first time."

Nick shakes his head. "But what about the doughboy? Come on, Anne, don't pull that one on me. I read World War II novels. It happens every time with them, sometimes even twice."

"You mean with David? Never."

"Never?"

"Never."

Vicky leans against her car and chatters her teeth. The December night is cold. "Well, well," she says, "I wasn't sure you were going to show."

Nick shrugs. "I figured it would be nice to swap stories. Remember the one about the girl who lived next door?"

"I made that up," Vicky says. "And if you want a ride you're going to have to tell me your name." They get inside her car.

"And I believed you," Nick says. "The name is Sandy Koufax."

"I'm Jayne Mansfield, and I'm cold and exhausted."

"Do you want to get some coffee?"

"No, let's just go to bed."

"I only pour the stuff, lady, I never touch it."

Vicky frowns, pulls out into the street, then lets her hand fall to his thigh. "But Nick," she says. Her tongue licks her bottom lip.

"But Vicky," Nick says.

Her fingers tiptoe toward his belt. "But Nick—"

"Vicky—"

She drives. "Why not? Don't you find me attractive, or did a line drive hit you where it counts?"

Nick smiles and leans back. "Because I think it would be wrong, that's why. Didn't they ever teach you that in school?"

The telephone crackles. "You're not serious, Nick," Anne says. "We're old enough for our own decisions. After all, we're seniors in college."

"I'm confused, Anne. I don't know what advice to give you."

"Well, I don't know what to do, Nick."

He takes a deep breath, looks at the receiver in his hand, then hangs up. Then Nick paces the room, hitting the walls of his basement apartment with his left fist. Then he goes into the kitchen and knocks over the table. He walks out of the pantry

with a Coke bottle and fires a sidearmed curve at the picture
tube of his TV. The blank glass shatters.

The phone rings and rings.

"Did you hang up on me?"

"I just busted up my apartment, Anne."

"Nick, I just busted up my life."

"But you're sure, Anne, you're *sure* it's not my child?"

Earlier, a full ten months earlier, during the spring of Nick's
junior year, on the tiny patch of grass near the Psychology
Building, Anne is telling Nick the identical thing, only this
time it *is* Nick's child. Nick holds his stomach and breathes
quickly through his teeth. Anne looks out at the street. Nesting
birds chirp. The sun dumbly shines.

"I feel like my life's just been stopped," Nick says.

"Well how do you think I feel?"

"I guess we'll have to get married."

"I don't want that. Not if it's like this."

"O.K. Give me an alternative. Do you want to raise the
baby yourself? Or do you want to put it up for adoption?"

Anne stares him full in the face. "I'll give you an alternative, Nick. Air fare. Kansas City. An abortion, damn it."

Nick says nothing.

"Well, Nick, I don't want to rush into getting married."

"What did the doctor say?"

"I haven't seen one yet."

"Well, let's get you to a doctor."

"Sure, Nick. A doctor."

"And let's think about this, O.K.? This is very serious."

Anne sighs. "Don't I know."

Nick holds his brow. "This changes everything," he says.
"I need time to think. Give me time to think." He takes a step
away, then turns. "Anne, please don't do anything until we
decide what's best for both of us."

"Sure, Nick."

He crosses the street and goes into Stan's Gridiron. A year of doing it, he thinks, and now this. Progenation. The law of averages. Another life. He shoves his way through the crowded bar, enters the john, waits for an open spot at the urinal trough, unzips. "You," Nick says aloud. "You've screwed up my life."

The guy standing next to him looks over. "Huh?"

"I said you screwed up my life."

"Eat it, meatball."

"Keep your eyes to yourself, fella."

A voice from inside one of the stalls. "Hey, if you two are fairies, go around the block to The Wigwam." Then the voice whistles.

Nick shakes and looks up, sees the guy hulking next to him. "You hear him in there? I'm having a conversation with my joint and he calls the two of us fairies."

"You was talking to your joint?"

"A girl I know just told me she's expecting." Nick spits and pounds his palm with his fist.

"Uh huh," the big guy says. The stall door opens. The whistler steps out. Nick steps back when the fight starts. For a while he watches.

Then Nick calls out. "Hey, give me a hand busting this off the wall." He points to the condom machine. The big guy grins.

"It's the machine's fault," Nick says. "You got the idea?"

The big guy nods and slams both fists against the machine's side. It creaks and wobbles. He slams both fists again. The whistler runs out, both lips bloodied, and Nick watches the machine as it falls, hears it smash against the porcelain of the urinal. He lifts it up and over his head and throws it inside the open stall. The big guy is on his knees, stuffing his pockets with quarters. Nick's breath is quick. He smiles and steps outside.

And walks out to the university's pastoral South Farms, his hands in his pockets, his heart in his mouth, thinking. His kid. *If* there is a kid. If there isn't a kid then there isn't a kid. Nothing to worry about then. But if there is a kid it's his kid. If there is a kid—

Nick pictures wastebaskets, green plastic garbage liners, red blood, and tiny hands and fingers. If there is a kid. Nick pictures Anne's legs, open and splattered with blood. He closes his eyes.

"It would be wrong, Anne. I don't think you should do it."

She breathes into the phone. "We're talking about my life, Nick."

"But you're sure, dead sure, this baby isn't mine?"

Vicky yawns and stretches out on the couch in Nick's apartment. Nick pounds the arms of his chair. "I could get another meteor easily," he says, "or would you prefer something more in the line of a sudden incurable disease? Imagine the remainder of your life spent wasting away in a hospital, Vicky. Yawn once more and you'll regret it."

"What are you talking about?" Vicky says.

"Just my life," Nick answers.

"But I want to go to bed. Can't we—"

"You can think of bed at a time like this?"

Her eyes widen as she nods.

"The world is quietly becoming insane and all you can think of is bed? Vicky, where's your character?"

Her hands begin unbuttoning her blouse. Nick shields his eyes.

"That comes close to violating good taste, Vicky."

"Yes, Nick. I'm certain the baby isn't yours." The television set is shattered.

"Have you considered entering a convent?"

"Nick, did you hit your head?"

"Anne, this is ripping my guts up."

"I've got feelings too."

"It's his baby, you're sure about that, and then you call me."

"But I can talk to you better than I can talk to him."

"But you can't marry me better."

"Nick, let's not go through that again."

"I know, I know. He's a first lieutenant with a future—a growing business, the Army—and I'm the wild man of the Big Ten, without a fastball or a scholarship, and this spring I'll probably be riding the bench."

"It's not just that, Nick."

"Anne, it is exactly that."

Nick stops by the barns and looks at grazing sheep. He sits on a fence and hangs his head, imagining himself rising and striding from the bullpen to the pitcher's mound. It is a fine bright spring afternoon. He looks around as he jogs out. He sees the box seats change to church pews. The bases are loaded with Anne's relatives. Nick tries to throw his first warm-up pitch, but the ball inside his glove is a wadded diaper. It floats to the infield grass, and he sees Anne slowly march down the right-field foul line with her father. Her belly looks like a balloon. He sees them kiss at first base. Anne kneels at home plate before the umpire. Nick is suddenly next to her singing the *Kyrie*. The stands are empty. Nick cries out. The sheep look up at him and bleat.

He walks from the South Farms back toward campus. He goes into Treno's and asks the bartender there for change. He takes a handful of napkins from the counter to disguise his voice, then enters the phone booth and unscrews the light bulb. Nick makes the sign of the Cross and begins dialing.

First his trainer, who might know about these things, Nick thinks, but whose wife says is out, and then Nick tries a guy he met during his first year in the dorms. Nick sits in the darkness of the tiny booth and taps his feet and sweats. He gets the number, dials the area code of Kansas City.

"I've, uh, I've got a friend who's got a problem."

"How long has she had this problem?" The voice is clean, professional. Very slick, Nick thinks.

"A little over two, uh, I think two months."

"Well, allow me to explain what your friend might do."

Nick pictures the voice sitting at a desk in a darkened room. Stubby fingers fondle the phone. The voice's teeth are yellow. In the hands is a fat cigar. The stubby fingers are yellowed. The breath is bad. Roaches run about on the floor. Nick thinks the voice is smiling, is laughing, was counting greasy money before he called. He hangs up.

And dials Anne's number.

"Beverly?"

"Yes? Hello? You'll have to speak up, I can hardly hear you."

Nick looks at the napkins over the mouthpiece, then throws them to the floor. "Bev, this is Nick. I need to talk to somebody."

They arrange to meet outside of Treno's. Nick walks out into the now cool evening air. He paces. He smokes a cigarette even though it breaks his training. He laughs. He looks at passing couples, counts cars, parking meters, the number of dark spots on the full face of the rising moon, then slaps his hands.

And begins running, full out, past Krannert, past the greenhouse, across the Quad and beyond the Student Union, across Green Street, dodging coeds and bicycles and buses and wheelchairs, to the field behind Men's Old Gym. Nick is crying, or it is the wind against his face, the feeling in his stomach, the run, and he slows, rubs his eyes, leans against the backstop and stares at home plate in front of him. He holds his sides and squats, then folds his hands, bows his head. He kneels, prays.

"You can look up now."

Nick squints between his fingers. It isn't a trick—her blouse is fully buttoned. Her legs are crossed. She isn't yawning.

"The incurable disease threat worked, huh Vicky?"

She smiles, then runs her hands through her blonde hair, stretching out again on the sofa.

"I've got problems, Vicky."

"Nick. Let's put them to bed."

Anne cries into the phone. Nick looks up, exhales, stands. The telephone cord is tied into knots.

"Stop crying," he says. "Pull yourself together."

"You've got to help me, Nick."

"Is it money?"

"David can pay for it."

"Then what do you want from me?"

"I don't know, I just want to talk. I'm so confused."

"Anne, we talked about all of this last winter when you decided you wanted to marry him. So why don't you call *him* up and cry on *his* goddamn shoulder? O.K., Anne? Leave me goddamn alone."

"Nick, I want you to understand something."

He is yelling. "Oh, I understand something. It's his baby, you're sure about that, or at least you think you're sure, or anyway you're going to marry him this spring as soon as you graduate and he gets his commission, and you call me first to tell me you need a goddamn abortion. Sure, Anne, I understand."

"Nick—"

"You made me break my TV set."

The field is dark, empty.

There are hits, Nick thinks, and there are outs. The altar versus the airplane. As a pitcher Nick knows he should prefer the latter—you need twenty-seven every game to earn the complete win. Got to get them when you can, in whatever way you can. He puts his hand inside his jacket pocket, takes out the long-distance telephone number.

Nick squats behind the plate, flashing the series of signs.

But if there is a kid, he thinks, the kid would be retired before he even came up to the plate. Killed before he was born. If you're a full-blown person then. If you're not, then it's no matter. You're hamburger. But if you are fully alive—

The visitors' dugout changes to Mary's side altar. Nick shivers and shakes. Anne would walk there at the end of the ceremony, then kneel and leave a bouquet of flowers. They could try to make the best of it. They could try.

"Hell," Nick says, "it wouldn't be the first time I've pitched with a man already on base." He stands, jogs to first. Relieved, he taps the bag with his toe and wind-sprints to second. Nick imagines the ball bounding past the outfielder and quickly tries for third. The coach's arms are windmilling, and Nick makes his cut and barrels toward home, his arms and legs pumping, his pulse pounding in his ears. He lowers his shoulders, he raises his arms and slides, his foot hooks home plate. Safe! The crowd is on its feet.

He stand and brushes the dirt off his pants. "I'm a father!" he shouts to the empty stands.

Then Nick walks to the bullpen, pulling up the zipper on his jacket. He rests on the bench, closes his eyes for a moment. Sleeps.

"Good morning," Bev says. "So this is outside of Treno's?"

Nick squints in the bright early sunshine.

"We looked all over for you last night, Nick. Then this morning Anne said, 'Let's try the field, maybe Nick is at the field.' "

"Where is she?" Nick asks, sitting up.

Bev points to her car. Nick smiles and runs.

"Anne." He pulls open the car door. "Listen, I've got great news."

"So do I," Anne says. "Last night I started my period."

Nick rubs his forehead, then looks around his apartment for a cigarette. He sees a pack lying on top of the empty console of his television. Inside where the tubes were he keeps a stringy philodendron along with his cap and ball and glove.

"So now you know everything," he says.

Vicky smiles and motions for a cigarette.

"I work downtown at the Art Institute," she says. "Did I tell you that, Nick? I'll have to wake up early in the morning."

"I kind of like you, Vicky."

"Maybe I'll be back tomorrow night."

Nick and Vicky are in bed, and Nick is thinking about meteors. He falls through the sky and screams. He sees the earth below and drops over it, looking for Fort Gordon, Georgia, for Urbana-Champaign. Nick shifts into third, pushes the accelerator to the floor. He pulls back, drops the banana peel on the marble steps. He burns and flames like the meteor, dropping gently down again.

Nick is yelling from the pitcher's mound for somebody, for anybody, to please track down the ball. Nick is crying into an empty phone in a suddenly lonely basement apartment. Then hs is standing and running and knocking over his refrigerator. Nick kicks Bev's car door, he feels like throwing up, he doesn't know whether to rejoice or put his fist through the windshield. Nick plots trajectories, frequents fruit markets, never honks his horn. He packs his broken TV and moves to Chicago, driving a rented van up old Highway 45 and listening to the Cubs on the radio. He goes out each morning for the newspaper, he reads the sports and then the obituaries, he speeds faster down the asphalt road, he loses his footing on the slippery peel, in a whoosh he spills through the brown and green treetops.

Vicky is smiling. Vicky is warm. Vicky isn't yawning.

"You didn't cry," Nick whispers.

"Why should I cry?" She pulls up the sheet.

"Because you should, Vicky. Because I need to know these things. I need to know everything."

"Nick, do you work tomorrow night?"

"I work every night. But I'll quit tending bar this spring. Then I'll try out for semi-pro ball." He laughs. "At least it will keep me in shape, ducking all the line drives and running back to the locker room."

Vicky smiles. Nick stares at his hands.

"I'll come by tomorrow after work, Nick."

Nick is still living the middle.

"You know," he says, "we all should have died that day."

"But you didn't," Vicky says. "Nick? Nick, you didn't."

He gets out of bed, walks to the kitchen, stares at the refrigerator. Then he goes over to his TV and puts on his cap and glove. Naked except for his cap and glove, he walks back to the bedroom and rocks in the doorway.

"I talked her out of the abortion, but she married him anyway." He looks in his glove and sighs. "I found that out from Bev. She said he took a bus up from Georgia and sort of surprised her. I had a shutout going that afternoon against Michigan State, but it was called on account of rain."

"Nick, come back to bed."

"He married her right in the middle of finals week. She must have been just starting her sixth month then. The day outside the Student Union was the last time I saw her. I never found out if it was a boy or a girl."

"Nick, you look stupid."

"Lady, I'm a ballplayer."

"You still look stupid."

"This is how ballplayers look."

"Let's sleep on it, Nick. You didn't die."

He takes off his cap, puts down his glove. He slips under the covers. Vicky is warm alongside him. He puts his arms behind his head and stares up at the ceiling. Morning light begins to fill the room.

"I didn't die?" he says.

"Nick, you definitely didn't die. Take my word." Vicky snuggles next to him, then kisses him on the cheek.

"I'm not dead?" Nick says.

"No," Vicky sighs.

He pictures Anne walking away from the Union, her arms full of books, her womb round and heavy. "Probably not," Nick finally says. In his mind Nick nods to Anne, then waves.

Nonna

She has seen it all change.

Follow her now as she slowly walks down Loomis toward Taylor, her heavy black purse dangling at her side. Though it is the middle of summer she wears her black overcoat. The air conditioning is too cold inside the stores, she thinks. But the woman is not sure she is outside today to do her shopping. It is afternoon, and on summer afternoons she walks to escape the stifling heat of her tiny apartment, the thick drapes drawn shut to shade her two rooms from the sun, the air flat and silent, except for the ticking of her clock. Walking is good for her blood, she believes. Like eating the cloves of *aglio*.

She hesitates, the taste of *aglio* on her tongue. Perhaps she is outside this afternoon to shop. She cannot decide. The children of the old neighborhood call out to her as she passes them. *Na-na!* The sound used to call in goats from feeding. Or, sometimes, to tease. Or is it *Nonna,* grandmother, that they call? It makes no difference, the woman thinks. The thin-ribbed city dogs sniff the hem of her long black dress, wagging their dark tails against her legs. Birds fly above her head.

Around her is the bustle of the street corner, the steady rumble and jounce of cars and delivery trucks, the sharply honking horns, the long screeching hiss of a braking CTA bus. The young men from the Taylor Street Social and Athletic Club

seem to ignore her as she passes. They lean against streetlight
poles and parking meters in the afternoon sun. One chews a
cigar; another, a toothpick. One walks in front of her, then
turns to the gutter and spits. The woman looks into their faces
but she does not recognize any of them, though she knows
they are the sons of the sons of the neighborhood men she and
her Vincenzo once knew. Grandsons of *compari*. Do they
speak the old language? she wonders. Like a young girl, she is
too shy to ask them.

One boy wears a *cornicelli* and a thin cross around his neck.
The gold sparkles in the light. Nonna squints. Well, at least
they are still Catholics, she thinks, and her lips move as she
says to herself *They are still Catholics,* and her hand begins to
form the sign of the Cross. Then she remembers she is out on
the street, so she stops herself. Some things are better done
privately. The boy's muscled arms are dark, tanned, folded
gracefully over his sleeveless T-shirt. The boy has a strong
chin. Nonna smiles and wets her lips in anticipation of greet-
ing him, but his eyes stare past her, vacantly, at the rutted
potholes and assorted litter lying next to the curb in the street.

She looks at what he stares at. He grunts to himself and
joins his friends. On the shaded side of Loomis is the new
store, a bookstore. The letters above the front window read
T SWANKS. Could the *T* stand for Tonio? she wonders. She
crosses the street. Then it should properly be an *A*. For Antonio. Anthony. Named for any one of the holy Antonios,
maybe even the gentle Francescano from Padova. Nonna always preferred the Francescano but never told anyone. He had
helped her to find many lost things. She believes that if she
were to speak her preference aloud she would give offense to
all the others, and what does she know of them—Heaven is
full of marvelous saints. Her lips whisper Padova.

The sound is light. Nonna enjoys it and smiles. She pictures
Padova on the worn, tired boot. Vincenzo called Italy that.
Nonna remembers that Padova sits far up in the north, west of

Venezia. She looks down at her black shoes. Italia. She was from the south, from Napoli, and Vincenzo, her husband, may he rest, came from the town of Altofonte, near Palermo, in Sicilia. The good strong second son of *contadini*.

A placard in the bookstore window reads FREE TEA OR COFFEE—BROWSERS WELCOME. Nonna is tempted to enter. She draws together the flaps of her black overcoat. She could look at a map of Italia if the store had one, and then maybe she could ask Mr. Swanks for which of the Antonios was he named. And what part of the boot his family came from, and does he still speak the old language. She does not realize that T Swanks might not be the name of the store's proprietor. She assumes that, like many, Swanks is an Italian who has shortened his name.

Beneath the sign in the window is a chess set. Its pieces are made of ivory. The woman stares at the tiny white horse. It resembles bone. She remembers the evening she and Vincenzo were out walking in the fields and came across a skeleton. That was in New Jersey, where they had met, before they came to Chicago. She thought the skeleton was a young child's—she flailed her arms and screamed—but then Vincenzo held her hands and assured her it was only an animal. Eh, a dog or a lamb, he had said, his thin face smiling. Digging with his shoe, Vincenzo then uncovered the carcass. It indeed had looked like a dog or a lamb. That was a night she would never forget, the woman thinks. And that smell. *Dio!* It had made her young husband turn away and vomit. But Nonna is certain now that what she saw in that field that dusky autumn evening had been a child, a newborn *bambino,* clothed only by a damp blanket of leaves. The Devil had made it look like a dog! New Jersey was never the same after that. She made Vincenzo quit his good job at the foundry. They had to go away from that terrible place. Nonna openly makes the sign of the Cross.

She knows what she has seen. And she knows what kind of

woman did it. Not a Catholic, she thinks, for that would have
been the very worst of sins. It had been someone without religious training. Maybe a Mexican. But there hadn't been any
Mexicans in New Jersey. Nonna is puzzled again. And all
Mexicans are Catholics, she thinks. Each Sunday now the
church is full of them. They sit to the one side, the Virgin's
side, in the back pews. Afterward they all go to their Mexican
grocery store. And what do they buy? Nonna had wondered
about that all during Mass one bright morning, and then from
church she had followed them. The Mexicans came out of
their strange store talking their quick Mexican and carrying
bananas and bags of little flat breads. Great bunches of long
bananas. So green—

Maybe Mexicans don't know how to bake with yeast.
Nonna realizes her lips are moving again, so she covers her
mouth with her hand. If that is true, she thinks, then maybe she
should go inside Mr. Antonio Swanks's new bookstore and see
if he has a book on how to use yeast. Then she could bring it to
the Mexicans. It might make them happy. When they kneel in
the rear pews, the Mexicans never look happy. Nonna shifts
her weight from foot to foot, staring at the little white horse.

But the book would have to be in Mexican. And it would cost
money, she thinks. She does not have much money. Barely
enough for necessities, for neckbones and the beans of coffee and *formaggio* and *aglio* and salt. And of course for bread.
What was she thinking about? she asks herself. Did she have
to go to the store to buy something? Or is she just outside for
her walk?

She looks inside the bookstore window and sees a long-
haired girl behind the counter. Her head is bent. She is reading. Nonna smiles. It is what a young girl should do when she
is in a bookstore. She should study books. When she is in
church she should pray for a good husband, someone young,
with a job, who will not hit her. Then when she is older, married, she should pray to the Madonna for some children. To

have one. To have enough. Nonna nods and begins counting on her fingers. For a moment she stops, wondering where she placed her rosary.

No, she says aloud. She is counting children, not saying the rosary.

Nonna is pleased she has remembered. It is a pleasant thought. Five children for the girl—one for each finger—and one special child for her to hold tightly in her palm. That would be enough. They would keep the girl busy until she became an old woman, and then, if she has been a good mother, she could live with one of her sons. The girl behind the counter turns a page of her book. Nonna wonders what happened to her own children. Where were Nonna's sons?

She hears a shout from the street. She turns. A carload of boys has driven up, and now, from the long red automobile, the boys are spilling out. Are they her sons? Nonna stares at them. The boys gather around the car's hood. One thumps his hand on the shining metal on his way to the others. One boy is laughing. She sees his white teeth. He embraces the other boy, then throws a mock punch.

They are not her sons.

She turns back. It is clear to her now that the girl has no children. So that is why she is praying there behind the counter! Nonna wants to go inside so she can tell the unfortunate Mrs. Swanks not to give up her hopes yet, that she is still young and healthy, that there is still time, that regardless of how it appears the holy saints are always listening, always testing, always waiting for you to throw up your hands and say *basta* and give up so that they can say heh, we would have given you a house full of *bambini* if only you had said one more novena. Recited one more rosary. Lit one more candle. But you gave up hope. The saints and the Madonna were like that. Time to them does not mean very much. And even God knows that each woman deserves her own baby. Didn't He even give the Virgin a son?

Poor Mrs. Swanks, Nonna thinks. Her Antonio must not be good for her. It is often the fault of the man. The doctors in New Jersey had told her that. Not once, but many times. That was so long ago. But do you think I listened? Nonna says to herself. For one moment? For all those years? My ears were deaf! Nonna is gesturing angrily with her hands. She strikes the store's glass window. It was part of Heaven's test, she is saying, to see if I would stop believing. She pulls her arms to her breasts as she notices the black horses. They stare at her with hollow eyes. Inside the bookstore the manager closes his book and comes toward the window. Nonna watches her close her book and stand, then raise her head. She wears a mustache. It is a boy.

Nonna shuts her eyes and turns. She was thinking of something— But now she has forgotten again. She breathes through her open mouth. It was the boys, she thinks. They did something to upset her. She walks slowly now to slow her racing heart. Did they throw snowballs at me? No, it is not winter again. Nonna looks around at the street and the sidewalk. No, there is no snow. But she feels cold.

Then they must have said something again, she thinks. What was it? Something cruel. She stops on the street. Something about—

The word returns. Bread.

So she is outside to go to the bakery. Nonna smiles. It is a very good idea, she thinks, because she has no bread. She begins walking again, wondering why she had trekked all the way to Taylor Street if she was out only for bread. The Speranza Bakery is on Flournoy Street, she says aloud. Still, it is pleasant today and walking is good for her heart. She thinks of what she might buy. A small roll to soak in her evening coffee?

The afternoon is bright, and Nonna walks up the shaded side of Loomis, looking ahead like an excited child at the statue of Christopher Columbus in the park. She likes the statue. Furry white clouds float behind the statue's head. Jets of water splash at its feet. She remembers the day the workers uncovered it. There had been a big parade and many important speeches. Was there a parade now? Nonna faces the street. There is only a garbage truck.

So it must not be Columbus Day. Unless the garbage truck is leading the parade. But it is the mayor who leads the parade, Nonna says, and he is not a garbage truck. She laughs at her joke. She is enjoying herself, and she looks again at the green leaves on the trees and at the pure clean clouds in the blue sky.

The mayor, she hears herself saying, is Irish. Nonna wonders why Irish is green. Italia too is green, but it is also red and white. The garbage truck clattering by her now is blue. So many colors.

She thinks of something but cannot place it. It is something about Italians and the Irish. The mayor. His name. He cannot be *paesano* because he is not from Italy. But she knows it is something to do with that. At the curb alongside her a pigeon pecks a crushed can.

It is Judas. Nonna remembers everything now. How the mayor unveiled the statue and then switched on the water in the fountain, how all of the neighborhood people cheered him when he waved to them from the street. All the police. Then the people were very angry, and the police held them back. Where did they want to go? Nonna thinks, then remembers. To the university, she says, to the new school of Illinois that the Irish Judas had decided to build in their neighborhood. The mayor's Judas shovel broke the dirt. And then, one by one, the old Italian stores closed, and the *compari* and *amici* boxed their belongings and moved, and the Judas trucks and bulldozers drove in and knocked down their stores and houses. The people watched from the broken sidewalk. Nonna remembers the woman who had tapped on her door, asking if she would sign the petition paper. The paper asked the mayor to leave the university where it was, out on a pier on the lake. Was that any place for a school? Nonna asked the woman. The woman then spoke to her in the old language, but in the Sicilian dialect, saying that Navy Pier was a perfectly good place. Then why build the school here? Nonna said. Daley, the woman said. Because of Mayor Daley. Because he betrayed us. Because he wants to destroy all that the Italians have built. First on the North Side, with the Cabrini Green projects, he drove us out. Now he wants to do it again here. He wants to drive us entirely from his city, even though we have always voted for him and supported his machine. Sign the paper. If you understand me and agree, please sign the paper. For a moment Nonna thinks she is the woman. She looks down to see the paper in her hands.

There is no paper. The paper had not been any good. The men in the street had told Nonna that. Shouting up to her windows, waving at her with their angry fists. She had yelled from her windows for them not to make so much noise. Two men tried to explain. Then what is good? Nonna had asked them. You tell me. I want to know. What is good? She is shouting. A car on Loomis slows, then passes her by and speeds up.

These, the men had answered. Rocks. Nonna is afraid again as she remembers. She had pulled her drapes tightly shut. But still from behind her open windows she had been able to hear all through the long night the shouts of the men who kept her awake and the rocks, rocks, rocks, thrown at the squad cars patrolling the streets and through the windows of the alderman's office.

She hears the water. Splashing up to the feet of Christopher Columbus, the boy who stood at the sea's edge thinking the world was round like a shiny new apple. Nonna knows history. She memorized it to pass the citizen test. Columbus asked himself why he first saw the tall sails of approaching ships, and then the apple fell from the tree and hit him on the head and he discovered it. Nonna is smiling. She is proud that Columbus is *paesano*. Sometimes when she studied and could

not remember an answer, she would hit herself on the head.
That knocks the answer out of sleeping, she says. Though
sometimes it does not, and Nonna thinks of her own head, how
once it had been full of answers, but now many answers are no
longer there. She must have lost them when she wasn't looking. Should she pray to Saint Antonio? But he helps only with
things, with objects. Maybe, Nonna thinks, when she puts
something new inside her head, something old must then fall
out. And then it is lost forever. That makes sense, she says.
She laughs to herself. It is the way it is with everything. The
new pushes out the old. And then— She puts her hands to her
head.

There is only so much here, she says. Only so many places
to put the answers. Nonna thinks of the inside of her head. She
pictures brain and bone and blood. Like in the round white
cartons in the butcher's shop, she says. The same. She makes
a face. All those answers in all those little cartons. Suddenly
Nonna is hungry. She wants a red apple.

A group of girls sits at the fountain's edge. Nonna hears
their talk. She looks at them, cocking her head. Did they just
ask her for an apple? Someone had been asking her a question.
I don't have any, she says to the girls. She pats the pockets of
her black coat. See? she says. No apples. She wonders what
kind of girls they are, to be laughing like that on the street.

They must be common, Nonna thinks. Their laughter
bounces up and down the sunny street. Like Lucia, the girl
who lives downstairs, who sometimes sits out on the steps on
summer nights playing her radio. Nonna often watches the girl
from her windows; how can she help it, the music is always so
loud. A polite girl, Nonna thinks, but always with that radio.
And once, one night when Nonna was kneeling in her front
room before her statue of the Madonna, she heard Lucia with
somebody below on the stairs. She stopped praying and listened. She could not understand any of the words, but she
recognized the tone, and, oh, she knew what the girl and the

boy were doing. The night was hot, and that brought back to
her the thin face of her Vincenzo, and she was suddenly young
again and back in terrible New Jersey, in her parents' house,
with young Vincenzo in the stuffed chair opposite her and
around them the soft sound of her mother's tranquil snoring.
Nonna shakes her head. She knows what she must feel about
that night. She was trusting, and Vincenzo was so handsome—his black curls lay so delicately across his forehead,
and his smile was so wet and so white, bright—and she allowed the young boy to sit next to her on the sofa, and she did
not protest when he took her hand, and then, when he kissed
her, she even opened her mouth and let his wet tongue touch
hers. Oh, she was so frightened. Her mouth had been so dry.
On the street now she is trembling. She is too terrified to remember the rest. But the memory spills across her mind with
the sound of the girls' easy laughter, and she moves back on
the pink sofa and does not put up her hands as Vincenzo
strokes her cheek and then touches her, gently, on the front of
her green dress. And then she turns to the boy and quickly
kisses him. The light from the oil lamp flickers. The snoring
stops. She looks at Vincenzo, and then she blushes with the
shame of her mortal sin, and now if Vincenzo does not say they
will marry she knows she will have to kill herself, and that in
God's eyes she has already died.

Nonna is still, silent, standing in her guilt on the street,
afraid even now to cross herself for fear she will be struck
down. She feels the stifling weight of her sin. Vincenzo then
moved back to the stuffed chair, coughing. Neither spoke. She
began to cry. The next morning Vincenzo spoke to her father.

There are boys at the fountain now, talking. Nonna looks up
from the crack in the sidewalk she was staring at. The girls sit
like bananas, all in a bunch. One of the boys flexes his arm
muscles, like a real *malandrino*. The girls look at him and
laugh. Nonna recognizes Lucia. She wears a tight pink top and
short pants. Why doesn't she hear Lucia's radio? Nonna won-

ders. A voice inside her head answers her question. Because
the girl is with the boys. And when you are with them, Nonna
says out loud, you do not need the radio.

They look up. Nonna knows she must avoid them. They
heard me, she whispers to herself, and now they will throw
apples at me. *Santa Maria, madre di Dio.* She feels awkward
as her feet strike the pavement. From behind she hears them
calling.

Nonna! Hey Nonna! Who were you talking to? Hey, Nonna!

Nonna begins to run, and as she does her heavy purse bangs
her side, up and then down, again and again. Then the sound
of their laughter fades away, and Nonna slows, feeling the
banging inside her chest. Now they heard, she thinks, now
they know my sin, and they will tell everyone. And then
everyone, even the old priests here in Chicago, will know. I'll
have to move to another neighborhood, she tells a fire hydrant.
I'll pack my pans and the Madonnina and flee. But I have done
that already two times. First, from New Jersey, and then when
I was punished by the machines who flattened my house down.
Nonna does not count the move from Naples, when her family
fled poverty and the coming war, nor the move from her parents' house when she married Vincenzo.

He would not have wanted her to be so lonely, she thinks.
She is lucid, then confused. Vincenzo understood why she
could bear no children; it was because of their sin. Perhaps
now that everybody knows, she thinks, she would not have to
move any more. Maybe since the whole world knows, I can
finally rest where I am now and be finished with my punishment. And then I'll die, Nonna says. And then, if I have been
punished enough, I will be once again with my Vincenzo.

Her legs turn the corner for her. They are familiar with the
streets. Nonna is on Flournoy, across from the church of Our
Lady of Pompeii. At first the building looks strange to her, as
if she were dreaming. The heavy wooden doors hang before
her inside a golden cloud. She walks into the cloud. It is the

blood in her head, the bone and the brain, she thinks. She pictures the fat butcher. The church's stone steps are hollowed, like spoons. Again she feels hungry. As she walks into the sunlight she wonders why she is wearing such a heavy coat. Nonna asks the doors her question. The doors stand high before her, silent. She pulls on their metal handles. The doors are locked.

She could go to the rectory and ask the priests for the keys. But they never give them to me, Nonna tells the doors. The priests tell me to come back for the Mass that evening, and I ask them if they don't think the saints and the Madonna are lonely with no one praying to them in the afternoon, and they say there are people all over the world who are praying, every moment of the day, but I don't believe it. If it was true, it would be a different world, don't you think? She presses her cheek against the wood. Don't you think? she says. Don't you understand me?

Then she hears something behind her and she turns. A dog. Panting before the first of the stone steps. Its ears are cocked. It is listening. Nonna laughs. The dog gives her a bark, and then from the middle of the park across the street comes the sound of a boy calling. He jumps in the sun, waving a dark stick. Nonna points to him. The boy is dark, like the stick. A Mexican. So it is a Mexican dog. And Nonna says, I would tell you that boy wants you, but I don't know Mexican, and if I spoke to you in my tongue from Napoli you would just be confused. The dog turns and runs, as if understanding. Again Nonna laughs. What is she doing at the top of the stairs? She knows the church is kept locked in the afternoon because of the vandals. Haven't the priests often told her that?

Her hand grasps the iron railing. She must be careful because of her legs. They get too tired from all the time holding her up. When she reaches the sidewalk she stops and faces the church and kneels, making the sign of the Cross. Then she walks again down Flournoy Street.

Why was I at the church? she thinks. She makes the sign of the Cross and then smiles as she walks past the rectory, and now she remembers the church-basement meeting she attended because of the paper she signed. It is good to sit with *paesani,* she thinks, and she pictures the faces of the neighborhood people, then the resolute eyes and mouth of the woman who gave the big speech. How much intelligence the woman has! Nonna notices that her hands are moving together, clapping. It is good to clap, good for the blood. She stops. But only in the meetings. The woman had said once and for all that it was the mayor's fault.

Vincenzo, Nonna whispers. She sees his still face sleeping on a soft pillow. His mouth is turned down into a frown. Vincenzo, I tell you, it was not your fault.

Nonna closes her eyes. She feels dizzy. It was the meeting, all the talk, the smoke. Then she realizes that was years ago, but she feels she had just been talking with her Vincenzo. Had he been at the meeting? No. Vincenzo died before the neighborhood changed. Before the students came. The *stranieri.* Before the Mexicans crept into the holes left by the *compari.* Then she must be walking home from Vincenzo's funeral. It was held at Our Lady of Pompeii. No, she had been driven to the cemetery in a long black car. Where is home? she thinks. Where am I walking to? And she pictures the faces of her parents, the rooms in the house in Napoli, the house in New Jersey, Vincenzo's house, the house in Chicago and the dust and the machines. Then—

Two rooms.

Nonna remembers where she lives.

So. She must go there. She worries that she has left something burning on the stove. Was it neckbones? Was that what she had taken out for her supper? Or was it meat in the white cartons? Had she bought brains? She cannot think. Her legs are very tired. She will eat, if it is time, when she gets home.

The color of the sky is changing, and the traffic grows more

The Evening News

heavy in the streets. It must be time, Nonna says to herself. She wishes to hurry so she won't be late. She does not like to eat when it is dark out. When it is dark she prays, then goes to bed. That is why there is the night, so people have a time for that.

Nonna approaches the street corner, and when she sees a woman coming out of a doorway with a bag full of groceries she remembers that she is out shopping. So that is why she has worn her heavy coat! But first she took a walk. The afternoon had been very nice, very pleasant. Did I enjoy myself? she thinks. It is difficult to decide. Finally she says yes, but only if I can remember what I am outside shopping for. What is it? It was on the tip of her tongue. What was it that she needed?

She turns at the door, and as she opens it she realizes that this is no longer the Speranza Bakery. It is now the Mexican food store. She is frightened. Her legs carry her into the store. The dark man behind the counter looks up at her and nods. Now she cannot turn around and leave, she thinks. She hopes the Mexican will not ask her what she wants. What would she say? Her feet move slowly down the first aisle. Her hands draw together the flaps of her coat.

Well, she thinks, I must need something. She does not want a can of vegetables, nor any of the juices in heavy bottles. She sees the butcher's case and tries to remember if she needs meat. Then she pictures neckbones in a pan atop her stove. She must hurry, she thinks, before they burn.

Cereal, vinegar, *biscotti* in paper boxes. Cottage cheese or eggs? Nonna's heart beats loudly when she sees the red apples, but she remembers how difficult apples are to chew, and she is too impatient now to cut them first into tiny pieces. Nonna smiles. Vincenzo had always said she was a patient woman. But not any longer. Not with hard red apples and a sharp knife.

Then she sees the bananas and, excited, she remembers.

What she needs is next to the counter. In plastic bags. Nonna is so happy that tears come to her eyes. So this is why she was outside, she thinks, why she is now inside this strange store. She had wanted to try the freckled Mexican flat breads. Hadn't someone before been telling her about them? Nonna holds the package in her hands and thinks. She cannot remember, but she is sure it had been someone. The woman with the petition paper, or maybe the girl who prayed for babies in the bookstore. Someone who explained that her punishment was nearly over, that soon she would be with her Vincenzo. That these were the breads that were too simple to have been baked with yeast, that these did not rise, round and golden, like other breads, like women fortunate enough to feel their bellies swell, their breasts grow heavy with the promise of milk, but instead these stayed in one shape, simple, flat.

The dark man behind the counter nods and smiles.

Perhaps, Nonna thinks as her fingers unclasp her purse and search for the coins her eyes no longer clearly see, perhaps bread is just as good this way.

Previous Winners of

David Walton, *Evening Out*
Leigh Allison Wilson, *From the Bottom Up*
Sandra Thompson, *Close-Ups*
Susan Neville, *The Invention of Flight*
Mary Hood, *How Far She Went*
François Camoin, *Why Men Are Afraid of Women*
Molly Giles, *Rough Translations*
Daniel Curley, *Living with Snakes*
Peter Meinke, *The Piano Tuner*